Wild Card

SUSAN HAYES

The game of love can change in a heartbeat when fate deals you a wild card.

Technician Lieksa Kiv saw firsthand what the corporations did to their cyborg soldiers during the Resource Wars. Her job: repair their damaged cybernetic components and send them back into battle. When a stolen kiss reveals the truth about her charges, Lieksa sacrifices everything to protect the cyborgs' secret, including a future with the two men she's fallen for.

Mack Darian and Dash Scudo aren't soldiers anymore. Inspired by the kindness of the woman who saved their lives and touched their hearts, they are defenders, instead. As Corporate Security, they're dedicated to protecting the citizens of The Drift from all threats, including each other.

When these three lives reconnect, the flames of passion burn white hot. But before they can hope for a future together, they must contend with old secrets and present-day challenges threatening to tear their world apart.

COPYRIGHT

Wild Card
Author: Susan Hayes

ALL RIGHTS RESERVED: This literary work may not be reproduced or transmitted in any form or by any means, including electronic or photographic reproduction, in whole or in part, without express written permission.

All characters and events in this book are fictitious. Any resemblance to actual persons living or dead is strictly coincidental. It is fiction so facts and events may not be accurate except to the current world the book takes place in.

DEDICATION

For my Mum and Dad, for supporting me even when they thought I was crazy. And for my best friend, Karen, for putting up with me when I was definitely nuts.

ACKNOWLEDGEMENTS

Thanks to Bianca Sommerland, for giving me the inspiration for a certain snowy scene.

SUSAN HAYES

Table of Contents

PROLOGUE

Out on the edge of civilized space lies a rag-tag collection of space stations and platforms known as the Drift. It's a haven for the hunted, the lost, and those seeking second chances. The ones who live there hail from every species, class, and corner of the galaxy, but they all have one thing in common: they don't belong anywhere else.

There's nothing beyond the Drift but wild space and an asteroid belt full of ore-rich rocks. Hundreds of mining vessels and their hard-working crews mine the asteroids. When the ships deliver their haul to be processed, those crews hit the infamous bars, casinos, and pleasure houses that are the Drift's primary source of income…and the only source of entertainment.

It's a world of its own. One where corporations rule, the laws are flexible, and everything is for sale, for the right price.

Welcome to the Drift.

CHAPTER ONE

"Lieksa! Where are you? Damn it, why aren't you answering your comm?" Her boss's bellows were loud enough to rattle the walls of her tiny workshop.

Officially, her workspace was Astek Corporation's Small Robotics Repair Laboratory, but the only one who called it that was the half-Torski male currently braying her name at the top of his lungs.

"I'm back here, repairing the service droid you said was a top priority because the stars might all go dark if the senior staffers had to go more than a few hours without their beloved robotic barista."

"Forget the *fraxxing* coffee-bot. You're needed at the med-center. They need your help with a patient."

Lieksa finally raised her head, sweeping back a few stray locks of her red hair from her eyes with a frustrated swipe of her hand. "A patient? You mean they need me to fix a piece of equipment, right?"

Zale's voice dropped to a fraction of its usual volume. "No, not equipment. You're going to be working on a cyborg."

Her heart froze mid-beat and her stomach clenched. She didn't do that kind of work anymore. She opened her mouth to remind him, but he cut her off with a wave of his four-fingered hand. "It's you or nobody. You're the only qualified engineer currently on the station. If you don't help, they're going to lose him."

That got her moving. She had enough blood on her hands already. "What am I dealing with?" Her mind was racing at light speed as she cataloged what she might need to treat a damaged cyborg and filled her toolkit.

"I don't know much. Patient was shot multiple times, and his cybernetic systems are damaged. His medi-bots and the doctor have patched up his body, but without repairs to his cybernetics, he won't make it. He's a Corp-Sec officer. They were doing a pharma raid, and things went sideways."

"That's it? No information on what components were damaged?" she asked, already falling back into old patterns. Assess the subject. Determine a course of action. Implement. The only difference was the last time she'd thought that cyborgs were nothing more than machines. Now she knew better. He was a human being, and his life was in her hands.

Zale shrugged his massive shoulders. "That's all I know. Hell, I think that's all the doctor knows. Everything about those poor bastards is still a carefully guarded secret. You probably know more about cyborg physiology than anyone in the Drift. This request came from the highest levels. It lit up priority codes I've never even seen before. According to the request, you've been re-assigned. Your only job for the next while is making sure that officer makes a full recovery. There's a Corp-Sec vehicle waiting for you at the main doors. They'll have more information for you, but you need to move your ass."

She grabbed a few more things off the back shelves, slung the bag over her shoulder, and jogged over to where Zale stood, his big body filling the entire doorway.

He stepped aside and dropped a hand onto her shoulder. "No matter what happens, don't blame yourself. You're already carrying enough guilt to have your own gravitational field."

She shook her head in denial. "Hardly."

Zale waited until she was halfway down the corridor before continuing, his voice back to its usual volume. "No one with your credentials would be down here in the bowels of corporate hell if they didn't have a reason. Either you're being punished, or you're punishing yourself. Since I know you've turned down two promotions, I'd guess it's the latter."

She slapped her hand on the call button for the elevator. "If that's true, then what are you down here for, boss?"

The silence stretched for so long she didn't think he would answer her at all. It was only as the elevator doors were closing that he spoke again. "We've all got our secrets. You tell me yours, maybe I'll tell you mine."

A bitter laugh tumbled from her lips as she rode up to the main level. If Zale ever found out her secret, she would lose her job. If her corporate employers ever learned what she had done, the only place she would find work was on the automated garbage scows or medical waste freighters making runs to dump their contaminated cargo into the heart of some distant star. Some secrets were never meant to be shared.

The door opened, and she took off at a run, ignoring the stares as she bolted through Astek Corp's crowded lobby and headed for the flashing lights of the corporate security team waiting to take her to the med-center.

* * * *

"Why can't you do it, Alyson? You're the best doctor out here." Mack Darian paced the worn tiles of the medical center's dingy hallway and tried not to think about the fact his best friend lay on the other side of the wall, unconscious and broken.

When Dash recovered, Mack was going to kick his ass for letting himself get shot...again.

Dr. Jefferies shook her head, her every move slowed by fatigue and worry. "I'd do my best, but it wouldn't be enough. I'm a doctor, Mack. I'm studying everything I can get my hands on, but I don't know enough about cybernetics or robotics yet to try and repair your partner. It would be irresponsible for me to even attempt it."

Mack didn't want to hear it. *Re'veth*, the last thing he wanted was for some clueless corporate lab-tech to get anywhere near Dash. They'd been patched up several times during their time in the Resource Wars, and only once had they been treated with any kind of compassion or skill. And then she had betrayed their trust.

He stopped pacing the grim, gray hallway of the medical center, his hands fisted at his side as he tried to keep his frustration in check. He avoided places like this: med-centers, robotics labs, anywhere that reminded him of the past. The antiseptic stink of this place had his nerves on edge and stirred dark memories he had no interest in revisiting.

"I don't trust anyone else, Doc. Not when it comes to him. Dash is my best friend, and I don't want one of those lab monkeys messing with him. They can't help themselves, they always end up *fraxxing* with things they shouldn't just to see if they can make it better."

"I'll be observing. I promise you, I won't let anything happen to Dash." Alyson fixed him with a pointed stare and squared her shoulders. "He might be your best friend, but he's also my patient. You're going to have to trust me, Mack."

"It's not you I have a problem with. It's those *fraxxing* techs. They have no idea how to treat us. No one does, because the corporations won't release our specs, and the ones who helped create us sure as hell aren't hanging out around this stars-forsaken place."

"You're wrong about that. There's at least one of us *fraxxing* techs in the Drift. Hello, Doctor Jefferies. My name is Lieksa Kiv. I'm from Astek's robotics division, and I'm here about the cyborg in your care."

He knew that voice. Soft tones, speaking Galactic Standard but with the accent of someone born on Earth. It was *her* voice. Denial and hope hurtled into each other with the force of a speeding comet.

Mack turned to find himself staring at a ghost. One look at the beautiful woman standing in front of him, and he was nearly buried under a tidal wave of memories and long-forgotten feelings. A different place. Another time. A face he never expected to see again, yet somehow, she was here.

"You're supposed to be dead," he blurted, half expecting the woman standing in front of him to disappear.

"So are you," she whispered back.

She was staring at him like he was the damned ghost instead of her, her glacier-blue eyes full of confusion and shock. *Veth*, she looked the same as he remembered her. Those petal-soft lips that had tempted him into giving up his greatest secret just for a taste. Her fiery red hair was pulled back into the same messy ponytail, and she still wore too-loose clothing to hide the sexy curves he'd explored time and again in his dreams. She was *here*.

Alyson cleared her throat. "I hate to interrupt this reunion, but if you don't get in there and repair my patient, he *will* be dead, unlike the two of you. I've stabilized him for now, but there's damage to his cybernetics I can't treat, including some to his cranial implants."

"Is it Dash? Hasn't he learned how to duck yet?" she asked.

"You don't get to make jokes, Lieksa. Not now. Fix him, and don't you dare tweak anything while you're doing repairs. You got me? Not like last time." He was torn between yelling at her and wanting to wrap her in his arms and never letting go. She was alive. Somehow, their angel was alive…and she had a lot to answer for.

Her eyes darkened with hurt, and she dropped her gaze to the floor between them. "I wouldn't do that. Everything's different now."

"You say that, but here we are again. We're still getting hurt in the line of duty, and you're still fixing us up like a good little corporate citizen. So, tell me what's changed?"

She started to protest, and he cut her off with a shake of his head as he pointed to Dash's room. "We'll talk later. Dash needs you."

"I will save him. You have my word."

He'd always liked the way she spoke, in soft, soothing tones that put everyone around her at ease. "You made me that promise once before, and you kept it. I want to believe you'll do it again."

Her lips lifted into a brief, bittersweet smile. "No, Mack. Last time I promised to save you *both*."

For a moment he thought she might reach for him, but instead, her smile faded and she turned to Alyson.

"What's Dash's condition? Do you have imaging of the injured areas? How are his medi-bots responding?"

The doctor replied with an almost nonsensical stream of medical terminology that made Mack's head spin. The litany continued until they entered Dash's room and the door sealed behind them, cutting off their conversation.

With a weary sigh, he wandered back to the bench where he had spent the last few hours and took out his data tablet. He wasn't leaving until he knew Dash was out of danger, but that didn't mean he had to sit around doing nothing. He had filed his initial report while Dash was in surgery. Now, he needed to figure out how the Drojo Cartel had known about today's raid.

First, one of his best informants had reached out to him, claiming to have important information, only to die of a pharma overdose mere hours before their arranged meeting. Now, they'd been ambushed. Only a handful of people knew about the plan, and every one of them was a vetted member of Corp-Sec. His gut churned at the idea that of one them working with the cartel. It was an unforgivable betrayal of trust.

Thoughts of betrayal brought his mind back to Lieksa. She was the first human he had ever trusted, and she'd abandoned them. How could she stand there and claim she had never broken a promise to him after what she did? He slammed a fist into the thinly padded bench, adding more bruises to his already battered body. His medi-bots would take care of the damage. That was their purpose. Microscopic nano-tech whose job it was to keep him healthy enough to go on fighting, no matter what.

Too bad they could only heal his body. When Lieksa had broken his heart, it had taken years to heal.

* * * *

Lieksa felt like her carefully constructed world had been shattered by a rogue comet strike. Her thoughts were tripping over each other, creating a bewildering tangle of questions she had no time to dwell on. She needed to stay focused. First, she had to repair Dash's implants. Later, she'd worry about fixing the shattered foundations of whatever the three of them had once briefly shared. If that was even possible.

Dash lay on the bed in the middle of the room, unconscious and surrounded by machines that hummed and chirped as they monitored his status. His wavy blond hair was stuck together in bloodstained clumps, and she could see the bruising that spread from the wound in his right shoulder. The injury itself was already healing. That was one of the challenges of working on the cyborgs. Their nano-tech healed them so quickly that repairing them usually involved reopening their wounds. Any suggestions about creating medi-bots that could be temporarily deactivated had always been denied by the ones in charge of the war effort. Their logic was always the same. Why create a weakness the enemy could exploit?

She took in everything the doctor was saying as she reviewed Dash's file, including images of the injured areas. There was definite damage to his implants, but it wasn't anything she couldn't repair. Once she did a thorough examination, she could have parts created by the 3-D printers back at her lab. Zale might not have her background in cybernetics, but he was a damned fine robotics engineer.

She had to put aside her emotions and do the job at hand. Later, though… later she was going to have a very large drink while she processed the fact that Dash and Mack were both alive, here on the

Drift, and at least one of them was convinced she had betrayed their trust.

Re'veth. What happened to her simple, quiet life? She'd come to the Drift to start over, to live small. Out here, no one cared about the past. Only the present mattered. It should have been the perfect place to get lost, but instead, it had brought her back into the orbit of the two men she had sacrificed everything to protect.

The doctor put a hand on Lieksa's arm. "Are you going to be okay to do these repairs? I don't know what the story is between the three of you, but it's obvious you have a history. As Dash's doctor, I need to know if you can do this. I won't put my patient in your care if you don't think you can. We'll find someone else."

Lieksa locked down her roiling emotions and met the doctor's gaze. There was no judgment in the blonde woman's eyes, only concern for her patient. "There isn't anyone else on the station that can do it. If there were, they'd be here instead of me. I don't normally do this kind of work anymore, but as it happens, I installed some of the implants I suspect are damaged. I'm probably the best person in the galaxy for this job. You can trust me when I tell you I can do this. I'll save him. I have to."

Dr. Jefferies nodded. "I needed to ask. I'm going to observe. I've been teaching myself everything I can about the cyborgs since I got here. I have several of them as patients. The more I know, the more I can help them."

"I'll be happy to explain everything I'm doing." Lieksa glanced toward the door. "Mack will want a full report afterward, anyway. You can update him after I've done an initial exam and determined what needs to be done. If I need new parts, I'll have them made at the lab and brought over. It's been a few years since I've worked on a flesh and blood patient, I'd appreciate your help when it comes time to make the incisions."

She looked at Dash again and felt a rush of sadness at seeing him this way, so quiet and still. He wasn't a quiet man. It wasn't in his makeup, or his programming. He was designed to gather information, which meant he was gregarious, charming, and heartbreakingly handsome. She was determined to make sure he'd be all of those things again, soon.

It wouldn't be enough to even begin to balance the scales, but it would be a good start.

CHAPTER TWO

Dash Scudo didn't need to open his eyes to know he was in a medical center—again. He recognized the sharp scent of antiseptic and the all too familiar beep and drone of nearby medical equipment. *Fraxx.* He was never going to hear the end of this from Mack or the other guys.

He cracked open one eye and bit back a groan as even that tiny movement triggered a stabbing pain in the back of his skull. He could temporarily block the pain, but before he did, he wanted to know how bad the damage was.

What the hell happened to him? He closed his eyes again and activated his digital recall to fill in the blanks. There was no playback. Nothing but a blank spot in his memory banks that spanned several hours. That shouldn't be possible. Nothing short of a headshot could inflict that kind of—oh *fraxx.*

He reached up and gingerly touched the side of his head where the pain was worst. A dressing covered the area behind his ear.

Somewhere nearby, a woman sighed. "If you poke at your injuries, they're going to take a lot longer to heal. The amount of times you've been shot, I'd have thought you'd figured that out by now."

Great. Now he was hallucinating. There was no way in the cosmos the owner of that voice could be here. He opened his eyes and lifted his head, earning himself a breathtaking dose of agony for his trouble.

"Damn it, Dash. Stay still! Dr. Jefferies and I didn't spend hours putting you back together so you could undo all our handiwork the second you woke up."

"Am I dead?" he asked as he stared into a pair of familiar blue eyes.

"Not yet, but if you keep letting yourself get shot, it's bound to happen eventually. How are you feeling?" she asked. The woman he'd once thought of as his angel was at his side, her hand on his chest as she tried to get him to lie down again.

"How am I feeling? Confused. If I'm not dead, then you're alive." He ignored the light pressure of her touch and tried to sit up completely, only to be hit with another wave of pain. "How—ouch! Exactly how many times was I shot?"

"Twice. You took one to the shoulder and one to the head. If I hadn't reinforced your skull-plate the last time, you wouldn't be here right now. Please lie down, Dash. You're not going to be getting out of that bed for a few days. Your injuries were severe."

The pain was bad enough that he took her advice. Once he was on his back, he sent a mental command to his systems to block all incoming pain and sighed in immediate relief.

"Why don't I have any recall of the last few hours?" he asked, while he tried to wrap his head around the fact she was here at all.

"Because your cranial implants were damaged. I've repaired them, but some data was lost. How many hours did you lose?" she asked.

Her clinical reply reminded him of the first time they met. It hadn't taken him long to realize her cool manner was a shield to protect herself from caring about her charges. She wasn't supposed to care. Techs weren't allowed to form any kind of connection to cyborgs. It was against the rules, and most of them had no problem complying. Not her, though. She had been different. Kinder. Gentler. He'd made it his mission to break through her armor that time. If she kept pushing him away, he would be tempted to do it again.

"How big is the gap?" she repeated the question.

"Data gap is thirteen hours, forty-two minutes, eighteen seconds."

She frowned. "Damn it, you lost more data than I was expecting. There's a gap between where your recall ends and when you were injured. I'm sorry, Dash. I was hoping to restore at least some of it. I know it's important. Mack might not be saying much to me right now, but he made it clear that the data could hold the answers to what happened."

"My turn to ask a question, now. How are you here? The ship you were assigned to was destroyed. All hands lost. We checked."

"I wasn't on the *Salan* when it was attacked. In fact, I wasn't even with Nobar Tech by then. I quit. It was the only way I could think of to protect you."

She removed her hand from his chest, and he reached out to capture it in his. There was no way he was letting her go. Not yet. "Why did you send us away? Do you have any idea what happened after you did that? We were still trying to get a handle on the modifications you inflicted on us, and suddenly we were back on active duty. We nearly died a half dozen times in the first month or so, until we finally learned how to turn the link off and on as needed. That wasn't protecting us. It was damned near a death sentence. I thought you cared about us, angel."

"I did care. More than I should have. More than was safe for any of us. I was trying to save you."

Her voice quavered with emotion, but he couldn't detect any sign she was lying. No microexpressions. No body language shifts. It didn't make sense. *Fraxx*, nothing made sense right now.

"What's your name? Your *real* name?" he asked. It was one of the reasons they hadn't been able to find her after the war was over. They had no name to hunt for, and the ship they had all been on had been destroyed shortly after they were transferred out. It was like looking for a needle in a nebula. They'd tried anyway, hoping for a miracle.

If only the rules had been different, they might have found her years ago, but the regulations were clear: technicians were to be referred to by their rank, and all cyborgs were to be referred to by their registration number. The same numbers imprinted on every cyborg's wrist.

"Lieksa. Lieksa Kiv." She offered him a shy smile that made her eyes crinkle a little in the corners. "It's nice to officially meet you, Dash. Now, I think you should let go of my hand so I can go tell Mack you're awake. He's been out in the hall since you came in. Said he wasn't leaving until he could see for himself you were okay."

Letting go of her hand was harder than he expected given what she had done to them. They had trusted her with the truth of what they were. Not machines, but men. Men who desired her and would have done anything to keep her. She gave them a taste of what they could have had, and then banished them back to the war without so much as a goodbye.

Fatigue washed over him and Dash gave into it, releasing her hand at last. "Send him in, but tell him to please hold off on the lecture until tomorrow."

"Dr. Jefferies already told him to take it easy on you. He's more likely to listen to her than to me right now, anyway. Try and get some rest. You need it."

"You're coming back, right?" He wasn't sure how he felt about her being back in their lives, but he was certain that now she was here, he didn't want her to vanish again. There were too many questions left unanswered. Too many things unsaid.

Lieksa turned to look back at him. "I'll be here until you're back on your feet. After that, I guess we'll have to see. A lot has happened since we saw each other last." She paused for half a heartbeat before adding. "I tried to find the two of you after the war ended, but Nobar Tech's records were in shambles after they were defeated. All I found was a partial list of registration numbers, including yours and Mack's. The ones I tracked down were all killed in combat. I thought you were gone, too."

He shook his head. "Mack and me, we're hard to kill. You should know, you helped make us that way."

She hung her head, wisps of her long, red hair falling around her face like a partial veil. "I didn't know, Dash. I believed what I was told. I thought you were machines. Once I knew the truth, I stopped. I swear that I haven't worked on another cyborg since. Not until today."

He closed his eyes for a second to gather his thoughts, but weariness slowed him down more than he expected. By the time he opened them again, she was walking out the door. He heard her voice in the corridor, and then Mack was there, looking equal parts relieved and annoyed.

"Do you have any idea how many reports I had to file because you let yourself get shot?" he asked, coming over to the bedside to glower down at him like he was a wet-behind-the-ears recruit on his first day.

"Nice to see you too, Mack. I'm fine, thanks for asking."

"I know you're fine. Doc's been giving me regular updates." Mack ran a hand through his dark hair, leaving it rumpled and messy. His red uniform was creased and unkempt, the fabric marked with darker red stains that looked suspiciously like blood.

"You hurt?" Dash asked, pointing to the stains.

"Me? No. That's your blood. I was trying to keep as much of it inside you as I could. I admit, I wasn't as successful as I would have liked. We nearly lost you and Len. He's in the next room, recovering from a shot to the chest. Those Drojo bastards knew we were coming. And we lost two more informants while you were out. Both dead of *crimson* overdoses. Someone's sending us a message, and I want to know who. I'm going to need all the data you gathered during the firefight so we can review it. Maybe it will give us something to go on."

"I don't have any of it recorded. The data was lost when I got hit. Lieksa said they damaged my cranial implants. I don't suppose any of it was relayed to you before I went down?" he asked and then answered his own question. "No, if it had, you wouldn't need my copy, you'd already have it. I can't even remember if I had initiated the link before I got shot. I'm missing too many hours of recall."

Mack stiffened the second he mentioned Lieksa's name. "Maybe she wiped it out herself. For all we know, she's working with them."

"You know that's not possible. If she were part of the cartel, we'd have known about her months ago. Wherever she's been hiding, whatever she's been doing, it's got nothing to do with the cartel." Mack was aware of that already. Mack was always aware of everything. They were created to complement each other's skill set. Dash got the data, and Mack analyzed it.

Mack grunted in acknowledgment. "She's been on Astek station for more than a year, Dash. A *fraxxing* year! She works for Astek, in the building half a block from the Corp-Sec office. *Our* office. We did miss her, which makes me wonder what else we've overlooked."

"Will you quit that already? I know what you're doing. You're preparing to go on an epic guilt trip. Don't even try.

The ambush wasn't your fault. We prepared. We followed protocol. If they knew we were coming, it's not because we screwed up. Stop trying to take the blame for this. Same goes for her. We thought she was dead. Why would we keep looking for a dead woman?"

"Maybe we should have. I don't know. I'm short on answers right now." Mack smacked a fist into his open hand. "She's got a lot of explaining to do."

"Yeah, she does." It was getting harder to think now, and Dash would have to sleep soon. "Promise me you won't go interrogating her on your own. When we talk to her, I want to be there."

Mack scoffed. "Afraid I'm going to be too hard on her and drive her away?"

"Yeah, I am. We had the start of something once. Something good. Since fate's put us back together again, don't you think we should hear her side of things?"

"We're not back together. We were never really together at all. A few hot kisses and some whispered promises in the dark of night do not constitute a committed relationship. If they did, you'd be the most committed man in the galaxy by now."

Dash shrugged, the slight gesture making his entire shoulder throb despite the pain block. "None of the others were her."

"Seriously? I'm going to tell the doc to check you over again. Apparently, she missed some brain damage. Ang—Lieksa sent us back into battle before we were healed, remember? She couldn't get away from us fast enough."

"I know. Same as I know that you haven't really looked at another woman since. Not to mention the fact she saved my life again. So, I'm going to give her the benefit of the doubt." He owed her that much. No matter what else she had done, she was the reason he was still breathing.

Right after Lieksa had given them the upgrades, the connection between himself and Mack had been a constant thing. Mack had been bombarded with a steady stream of input from Dash, seeing and hearing everything his partner did. The double dose of information was a distraction that very nearly got them both killed until they learned to control it. What no one else knew was the information relay wasn't only one way. Sometimes Dash got flashes of what Mack was experiencing, too.

Mack shook his head. "I'm not sure I can give her that much. But I won't talk to her until we can do it together. You look like death on toast, my friend. Get some rest. I'll be back tomorrow morning to check in."

"You don't look so hot yourself." Dash raised his hand in farewell. "Sleep well and don't stay up obsessing about what happened today. Any of it."

"I'm not taking advice from the fool who got himself shot twice in one day. Good night."

"Night, Mack."

He paused at the doorway, glancing back to Dash with an unreadable expression on his face. "I'm glad she was around to save your life."

"So am I."

Once he was alone, Dash closed his eyes and let himself drift into the welcome relief of sleep. His last thoughts were of Lieksa. What was she doing right now? Where was she, and where the hell had she been in the years since they had last seen her?

* * * *

By the time she got back home, Lieksa was almost drunk with exhaustion. It took her three tries to get her passcode entered correctly, and once the door opened, she staggered into her small residence cubby with a groan of relief.

"Cubby. Lights on, and activate the shower. Setting three," she instructed the rudimentary AI system that oversaw her tiny household. A single light came on, and she swore under her breath when she heard the telltale buzz and pop of another blown light fixture. She'd have to fix that tomorrow. If she attempted it in her current state, she would most likely electrocute herself.

Sleep was a priority, but only after she showered. There was no way she would be able to rest until every trace of Dash's blood was scrubbed off her skin. She stripped off her clothes, nearly tripping when she tried to take off her pants before her shoes.

Veth, she was a walking hazard right now, which wasn't surprising given she had been awake for more than twenty hours. She left her clothes on the floor and headed for the closet-sized space that was her bathroom. The shower was running, and steam billowed out as the door opened, wrapping her in its fragrant warmth.

Once she was standing under the scalding spray, her movements quickly became automatic. Soap. Water. Scrub. Repeat. Released from the need to focus on every decision and movement, her thoughts began to wander. It didn't take long to conjure up memories of the last time she'd seen Mack and Dash. The night that changed everything.

It was circumstance that brought them together. Both men had needed cybernetic repairs, and she was the one assigned to do the work. She quickly recognized their unique pairing made them the perfect test subjects for an experimental upgrade. Once they recovered from the injuries that brought them to the hospital ship, *Salan*, she had slated them for another surgery, this one with the express purpose of installing experimental implants and software.

She performed the upgrade herself and stayed with them until she knew they were both alright, regulations be damned. During the time it took for them to recover from their initial injuries she got to know them both, and she had come to care for them more than she should have.

She even knew their given names and used them when no one was around to hear.

She had dozed in a chair in their shared room while they recovered, wedged between their beds so she would be able to respond to any problem that arose. Dash had groaned, bringing her to his side in an instant. None of the readouts showed anything concerning, but she stayed where she was, watching him as he slept. Seeing him like that, asleep and vulnerable, it had been impossible to believe he was a killing machine and not a living being.

She hadn't heard Mack get out of bed. She didn't even know he was awake until suddenly he was behind her, his strong arms wrapped around her waist. Even now, years later, the memory of his touch made her breath catch in her throat, and she remembered the way his voice had rumbled in her ear.

"Do you want to know what he's dreaming about, angel?"

"Mack? You're awake. That's good, but you need to let go of me."

"What if I don't want to?" he asked, his voice still husky with sleep and his words slightly slurred by the heavy doses of drugs they had pumped into his body.

She liked being in his arms. The way his big body curved around hers, holding her so close she could feel the hard planes of his bare chest pressed to her back. It was common knowledge that some of the other techs indulged in recreational sex with the cyborgs, but she never had. It didn't feel right to her to use them that way. She'd never even been tempted. Not until tonight.

"You have to let go. I'm giving you a direct order. Release me, right now," she'd uttered the command with complete confidence that he would obey.

"No."

His refusal caused a flutter of panic deep in her gut. From her first day she had been told that no cyborg could refuse a direct order. Not even to save their own life. "Let me go."

Instead of releasing her, his arms had tightened, locking her in place. "I don't want to. I want to hold you and tell you what Dash is dreaming about. I know, because I can see it. Whatever you did to us, it's working. I can see his dreams, and they're all about you."

"Me? He's dreaming about me, and you can see it?" she asked, so distracted by his revelation she momentarily forgot he had refused a direct order.

"I can see and hear it like it's really happening. We've got you pinned between us while we strip off your uniform. Kissing, touching, and tasting every part of you. You're moaning our names, and it sounds good. I need to know what you taste like. Will you give me that much?"

Duty warred with want, and for the first time in her life, duty lost. Looking back, she still couldn't understand what had possessed her to trust him.

But in all the nights since, she had never regretted her choice. "Yes."

He groaned and turned her in his arms so that she was facing him. The moment she looked into his eyes, she knew. His hazel eyes gleamed with desire and so much more than that. This was no machine. He was a man. A man who wanted her.

His hand cupped her chin, tipping her head back as he lowered his lips to hers. "You're..." she whispered, too stunned to even finish her sentence.

"I am." He kissed her then, gathering her into his arms so that she could feel every inch of him pressed against her. He speared his fingers into her hair, his lips demanding as he devoured her mouth with his.

Behind them, Dash groaned. There was a note of hunger to it that made Lieksa's pulse quicken.

"I should check on him," she whispered, grasping at the last shreds of her control.

"No need. He's fine," Mack told her, a hint of laughter in his voice.

"Hello, angel. Am I still dreaming?" Dash murmured, moving in behind her and capturing her between the two of them exactly the way Mack had described.

"If you are, then you better not wake up anytime soon, my friend. I'm not ready to let her go." Mack lifted his head to smile at Dash, the harsh set of his mouth softening for the first time, making him appear so much more human.

"Who said we're letting her go?"

"Uh, says me." She'd finally found enough of her scattered wits to be able to speak.

Dash buried his face in the crook of her neck before answering. "Nu-uh. You've been bossing us around since we got here. It's our turn."

"I can't. I need to understand. You've got free will? Both of you? How long have you been like this?"

Instead of answering her, Dash spun her around to face him and silenced her with a kiss so fierce she could still feel the heat of it, even now.

An annoying chime began to sound, tearing her out of her daydreams with a strident alert that she had nearly exhausted her supply of hot water. The caress of water and steam was empty after the remembrances of their touch, and she shut off the shower with a tired sigh. It was a memory she revisited often, but it always ended the same way. Soul-searing kisses, and their promise that when the war was over, they would find her. But that wasn't what happened. To protect their secret, she sent them away. She'd had to. What they had revealed to her while they were drugged and vulnerable would get them killed, or worse. If their new upgrades continued to perform beyond the design team's expectations, Mack and Dash would have become test subjects under constant surveillance. It would only be a matter of time before the tests uncovered their secret.

Cyborgs were never supposed to become fully self-aware. They were soldiers in a bloodless war, manufactured pawns to be moved across a battlefield, nothing more. If the corporations learned that Dash and Mack were not only aware, but capable of defying orders, they'd tear them apart to find out what went wrong, and then they'd hunt down and destroy any other cyborgs who showed the same ability. She couldn't let that happen.

She filed a report declaring the upgrades a failure and ordered both men back to active status. The research and development teams were constantly testing new upgrades; some worked, some didn't. They'd just try again. No one would question her findings.

It defied logic, but the safest place for Mack and Dash was back in battle, where at least they had a chance at survival. The hardest part was not getting to see them again. She couldn't risk it. There could be no goodbyes or explanations that could raise suspicions. They had to go, quickly, before anyone suspected. It was the hardest choice she made that day. Resigning her job and walking away from her life's work didn't hurt as much as leaving behind the only men to ever touch her heart.

Until today, she thought it had all been for nothing. That they had died in the Resource Wars without ever getting a chance to be free. Now, she knew differently, but she also knew how they felt about her. She'd heard the bitter anger in Mack's voice when he'd told the doctor he didn't want a tech working on Dash. She'd seen the accusation and judgment in their eyes. They blamed her, and maybe they were right to.

She couldn't regret what she had done, though.

They might hate her for the rest of their lives, but at least they had lives to live.

CHAPTER THREE

Dash had been stuck in medical for two days now, and he was about to lose what was left of his mind. His body was healed, but neither the doctor nor Lieksa would release him until they were certain that his implants were all fully functional. He always thought it would be fun to have two women team up on him while he was in bed. Turned out, the reality wasn't anything close to the fantasy.

"Please tell me that's the last of the tests, and I can get out of here now," he said to Lieksa as she signed off on yet another form on her data tablet.

She glanced up, her ice-blue eyes gleaming with amusement for a moment. "Not yet. And if you don't quit moving around, I swear I'm going to put you in restraints. Be patient, my patient."

"Did you just offer to tie me up? I'm game if you are."

She blushed and shook her head. "No, I didn't. Well, I did, but that's not what I meant, and you know it."

"I live in hope," he replied with a wink. With little else to do, he had spent the last few days working on charming Lieksa out from behind her wall of cool, professional reserve. She seemed determined to keep her distance, which wasn't easy given the amount of time they spent together. Tests took time to run, and if she got a result she didn't like, she immediately ran a retest. Dr. Jefferies was almost as bad, but at least the medi-bots in his blood were doing most of her job for her. She would come in, look over the readouts, tell him to rest, and leave again.

Lieksa's reaction to his last comment was instantaneous. Her eyes darkened to a stormy blue, as if a cloud passed over the sun. All the light and warmth in her expression vanished. "You shouldn't say things you don't mean. I'm aware that flirting is encoded into your DNA, but I know how you two feel about me, Dash. Mack's made it very clear."

He winced. Mack's concern over the ambush, the rising body count of their informants, and a potential leak in their task force had his partner in a black mood, and he was taking out his frustration on everyone around him, including Lieksa. Confidentiality forbade them from explaining what was going on, so it made sense she thought his partner's frustration and anger was directed at her.

He was going to have to tell Mack to get a grip on his grumpy self before he ruined any chance they might have with Lieksa. If they had any chance at all, that is. It was too soon to tell. There had been no time to talk to her about anything important, yet. He was busy getting better, while Mack was running their task force singlehandedly.

The task force had originally been formed to deal with *crimson,* a new psychotropic drug that had appeared on the Drift a few months ago. An unlicensed pharma, it was harmless in small doses, but potentially deadly to anyone who overdosed on the vials of sweet, red liquid. Overdoses could lead to destructive rages, violence, and eventually death.

Four months after the first overdose, the team was no closer to ending the influx of *crimson* onto the Drift. They knew who was responsible, and their mandate had been expanded to include the apprehension and disbanding of a gang of thugs and drug runners known as the Drojo Cartel. This last raid should have put a few nails in the gang's coffin, but instead, it had been an ambush that could have taken down the entire team. Someone had targeted the task force, someone with inside information, and they had no idea who the traitor was.

"Mack's not angry with you. He's dealing with a lot right now. Two of his team were injured, and now, either all of our informants have suddenly developed pharma addictions, or someone is killing off our sources by overdosing them on *crimson*. It's a bad situation, and I'm not there to help him."

She scoffed. "You're wrong. He won't even speak to me now that you're recovering. All I get from him are dirty looks. I heard him talking about techs the night I came here to treat you. He doesn't trust any of us, most especially not me."

Frustration at their situation put an edge to his next words. "Can you blame him? You don't know what it was like for us. You were our angel of mercy. You had our lives in your hands, and suddenly you were gone. Thanks to the drugs you dosed us with we both *fraxxed* up and revealed something we shouldn't have. Then, before we can talk to you about it, we're back on active duty. We had no idea what was happening or why. Those first few days we were half convinced you were going to turn us in."

Lieksa recoiled as if he'd slapped her. "I would never betray you. I wanted to believe that you shared your secret with me because you trusted me…and maybe even wanted me enough to take that chance. Turns out that wasn't it at all. You two were just high and horny. My mistake."

She turned on her heel and fled the room, but not before he saw the shimmer of tears in her eyes. *Re'veth*, so much for fixing things. He'd just doused their chances in rocket fuel and set it on fire.

* * * *

Lieksa pulled herself together as she left Dash's room. She was not going to lose it in the middle of the medical center. This wasn't the time or the place, and she'd be damned if she was going to let anyone see how much their rejection hurt.

Zale had contacted her this morning, and she couldn't help but recall what he'd said. Officially, he had called to let her know that the higher-ups wanted her back in her workshop. The backlog of work was growing, and they expected her to finish up with Dash soon. Unofficially, he was worried about her and said as much. It was a vid call, so there was no way to hide her fatigue. He'd ended the call with a bit of unsolicited advice, and she could still hear his deep voice as it replayed on an endless loop through her mind. "Given your past, I don't think spending time with cyborgs is the best thing for you."

Yesterday, she would have hoped he was wrong. That maybe she could finally move past what she had done, and what she had lost. Today? Today, she agreed with Zale. She'd spent years trying to atone for what she'd done to the cyborgs. It didn't matter that she hadn't known her subjects were sentient. Guilt still gnawed at her. She had hoped that she could explain her actions to Mack and Dash. She wanted their understanding, but all she got was anger. Maybe that was all that she deserved.

"Everything okay?" someone asked.

She snapped her head around to see that Len Daniels, the other Corp-Sec officer who had been injured the same night Dash, was standing at the door of his room at the end of the hall. Len was human, which meant that despite the medical center's advanced technology, his recovery would be slow. He probably shouldn't be out of bed yet, but it wasn't her place to tell him so.

"It's fine," she said, hoping he didn't call her on the obvious lie.

"Nothing's wrong with Dash, is it? You just look a little stressed is all, and I know he was hurt pretty bad. You've been in and out of his room a lot. You his girlfriend?"

His last question caught her off guard "Girlfriend? *Veth*, no. Nothing like that. I'm the technician who repaired his damaged implants, that's all."

Len's ginger-colored brows raised in surprise. "I didn't know there was anyone around who could do that kind of work. Guess it was a good thing for him you were here, huh?"

"The universe was looking out for him. It sounds like it was watching over you, too. You took a blast to the chest, and you're still with us." She didn't want to talk about Dash right now. He was probably wishing it had been anyone else in the galaxy who had shown up to repair him.

Len nodded and gently touched a finger to the thick bandages she could see under his shirt. "The doc said I was lucky. My body armor took the brunt of the damage. Still, it's going to be a while before I get out of here." He gave her a lopsided smile. "Have pity on a wounded man and come visit me sometimes? The company of a pretty woman would do wonders for my morale."

"You want me to visit you?" she asked in surprise.

"Uh huh. You could call it your good deed for the week. I don't know if you've noticed, but this place isn't all that entertaining. We could talk, play cards, a game, whatever you want. It would be great to have someone to talk to. Please?"

It was nice to hear that someone actually want her company. Dash and Mack certainly didn't. She was going to be around the med center for a day or two more, anyway. She saw no reason to say no. "Okay. I'll even see if I can find a deck of cards. I'm Lieksa, by the way."

Len grinned. "Great. I'm Len, but I bet you already knew that. Time for me to get back to bed. If the doc catches me on my feet, I'll get another lecture. Come see me anytime."

He winked, then looked past her. "Hey, Mack. Come to check up on your partner?"

"Came to check on both of you. Do I need to order you to get your ass back to bed? We need you back on active duty, Len. Rest up."

"Yessir." Len snapped off a jaunty salute. "I'll see you later, Lieksa?"

"Later," she agreed.

Len went back into his room, leaving her alone with Mack. She turned and found him glowering at her. "Dash is—" she started to speak, but he raised his hand.

"How do you know Len?"

"I don't. I ran into him when I left Dash's room. He seems nice. I guess he doesn't know how you and Dash feel about me. Once he does, I'm sure he'll start giving me the cold shoulder."

"You have no idea how I feel about you. We haven't had a chance to talk yet," Mack pointed out.

His tone was softer than she expected given his furrowed brow and the set of his jaw, but it didn't change anything. She knew how they felt. "Dash already said everything there was to say."

"He talked to you already? *Veth*, we agreed we'd do it together."

Mack scrubbed a hand over his face. He hadn't shaved yet today. His uniform was fresh, but the man wearing it wasn't. Whatever he'd been doing between visits to the medical center, he hadn't been spending it taking care of himself. Not that she should care, but somehow, she still did.

"I guess he didn't think you needed to be there," she said, forcing a casual note into her voice.

"Apparently not." He scowled. "Wait, if he talked to you already, why were you out here flirting with Len?"

"Flirting?" She flung the word back at him dripping in venom. "I wasn't flirting with anyone. That was how normal people communicate with each other. We smile. We say nice things. We don't growl insults and bark orders. And even if I was flirting, why would you care? You two never cared about me. I was a drug-fueled mistake you both regret."

Fury darkened Mack's eyes and made him look downright terrifying, but she didn't move away. She was too angry to be intimidated.

"What the *fraxx* did he say to you?" he demanded. "Stay here. I mean it, Lieksa. Don't go anywhere until I've talked to Dash."

"And there you go again, barking orders at me. The war's over, Mack. You're not a soldier anymore, and I never was."

She turned her back, hoping to make it clear she was done with this conversation. They had said everything there was to say already.

A door opened, and she knew he was going in to see Dash. She held her breath, waiting for the door to close, but instead, Mack spoke again.

"Lieksa, please don't leave until we've had a chance to talk."

She stayed quiet, too confused to answer. The door slid shut again a few seconds later, and she released the breath she had been holding. He was gone for now.

"I didn't know he even knew the meaning of the word. I've never heard him say please before,"

Alyson's voice broke the silence that filled the corridor.

Lieksa turned to face the doctor, who was outside breakroom door with a fresh cup of coffee in her hand. "Sorry about that."

"Don't apologize. This is a place of healing, and judging by what I just heard, I'd say you three still need a fair bit."

"I'm not sure there's enough medical know-how in the universe for that."

"In my experience, everyone and everything heals, eventually. It just takes the right treatment." Alyson glanced around as if confirming they were alone. "And speaking of treatments, I was hoping to talk to you about an issue some of my cyborg patients are dealing with. I know you specialized in cybernetic systems, but did you ever come across anything about cyborg fertility?"

Mack and Dash weren't the only cyborgs on the Drift. Alyson was doing all she could to learn how to treat them, and Lieksa had already agreed to teach her. Someone needed to look out for the cyborgs, and experience had shown that the corporations couldn't be trusted to put anyone's best interests ahead of their own. Lieksa didn't think twice before answering. "Fertility? Not really. But if you tell me what the problem is, maybe I can find a way to help."

* * * *

Mack walked into Dash's room intent on finding out what the hell was going on with Lieksa. He hadn't missed the shadows in her eyes or the pain that fueled her angry words. "What in starsfury did you say to Lieksa?"

Dash touched a finger to his lips. "Quiet. She's talking to Alyson, and I want to hear what they're saying."

Mack shrugged and took a seat. Dash didn't use his intel gathering abilities lightly, especially not when it concerned friends. If he wanted to eavesdrop, then there was a good reason for it. "How long have you been listening?"

"Since I heard you barking orders at her."

"Not my finest moment. Loop me in?"

A brief nod from Dash was all the warning he got before his partner opened the connection between them. This was the experimental upgrade Lieksa had given them, and it had strengthened the bond between them in ways none of them had expected.

Lieksa's voice sounded in his head, as clear as if she were standing next to him. "...if you tell me what the problem is, maybe I can find a way to help."

"I've got three female cyborg patients, all of whom have given me permission to speak to you in hopes you can shed some light on their condition."

He knew about Cynder's situation already.

The corporations had done something to the female cyborgs and then lied about it.

Something that made it impossible for them to get pregnant. Despite more than two months' work, the doctor was still at a loss as to how to reverse what had been done.

He listened as Alyson explained in detail to Lieksa, and it occurred to him that the doctor trusted Lieksa more than he did. It was an uncomfortable revelation; one that left him with a knot in his stomach. In his mind, she'd wronged them, and he had treated her that way without giving her a chance to explain herself. It was time for him to do better.

If she gave him the chance, that is.

"I never heard about a program like this, but I was on a hospital ship. It was my job to put them back together and send them back into battle." Lieksa's voice broke a little as she added. "I quit the day I found out I wasn't working on machines at all. Mack and Dash...they showed me the truth. I thought it was because they trusted me. Once I knew, I left. I wasn't with any corporation when the war ended."

The doctor sighed. "I figured it was a long shot, but I had to ask. I hate not being able to give these women any answers, you know?"

"I can't imagine how they must feel. The corporations took so much from them already. I don't have the answers you need, but maybe I can get them. I work for Astek, I've got a decent security clearance. If you can write down the terminology I should be looking for, I'll see what I can dig up."

"Like hell she's digging for anything in Astek's files. If they catch her…" Dash grumbled, his expression stormy.

"From what she said to me outside, I'd say we would have a better chance of stopping a star from going nova than getting her to listen to us right now. What the *fraxx* did you say to her, anyway?"

Dash closed the connection between them, and there was a disorienting moment as Mack adjusted to being alone inside his head again.

"What did I say? A bunch of things I regretted the second I said them. And before you go blaming me for this mess, I'll point out I was trying to defend the lousy way you've been treating her when it all went sideways."

"Well, clearly that went well. Next time how about you let me own my stupidity instead of compounding it with yours? I thought you were the one gifted with god-like charm and charisma?"

"Compared to you, I am."

"Says the guy who just hurt Lieksa," Mack shot back.

"Which is at the top of the list of things I regret right now. That's not going to be enough to fix this, though, is it?"

"Nope." Mack ran a hand through his hair, sweeping it off his face with a groan of pure frustration. "To be honest, I'm not even sure what we're trying to fix. I've been so busy dealing with the fallout from the ambush and the overdose deaths, I haven't had time to process the fact she's here, alive and well."

Dash arched a blonde brow. "Bullshit. You had the time if you wanted to take it. I know you, Mack. You buried yourself in your work because it was easier than dealing with this—with her." He waved his hand in Lieksa's general direction.

He grunted. "Maybe."

"I stand by what I said before. We owe her a chance to tell her side of the story."

"Agreed." That much, Mack could agree to.

"So, any ideas on what we do now? Apart from apologize. I think that's a given."

"I have no idea," Mack admitted.

"You're the analyst, think of something!"

Mack rolled his eyes. "And you're the one programmed in seduction, infiltration, and charm. Why is this my job, again?"

"Give me a second, and I'll think of a reason."

Female voices in the hallway announced that they were out of time. He needed to get out there and say something before Lieksa decided to walk out of their lives again.

He didn't make it to the door before it slid open. Surprise and relief filled him when he saw she hadn't left at all. She had come to them. It was a good sign, and probably more than they deserved.

She took two steps inside the room and stopped, crossing her arms over her chest and fixing them both with a cool stare. "You asked me not to go until we talked. So, here I am. Talk."

Time to step into the comet's path and see what survived impact. "I owe you an apology. I haven't been fair to you. In fact, I've barely been civil. I'm sorry, Lieksa."

"And so am I. *Fraxx*, am I ever." Dash got out of bed and stood next to him. "I'm sorry. I didn't mean what I said."

"You said the only reason you two kissed me was because you were high on medications, and you regretted it. Did you think I was going to be okay with that? I gave up everything to protect the two of you. I quit my job that night and swore to never work on another cyborg. I couldn't. Not once I knew the truth."

She dragged in a ragged breath and kept talking, her words spilling out over each other in a torrent. "I kept your secret until the war was over. Then, I testified on behalf of your brethren, attesting to the fact I knew of at least two self-aware cyborgs who were on active duty during the war. My account was sealed, because if the corporations ever found out who wrote it, I'd be blacklisted. I thought you were both dead, and I *still* kept my promise."

"You testified? You were one of the anonymous witnesses?" Dash asked.

"I did. I was."

The need to reach out and comfort her overcame him, and Mack took a step toward

Lieksa, stopping short when he saw the doubt and hurt that still lurked in her eyes. He'd put that pain there. Given her reason to doubt them.

He was an idiot.

"Can we try again?" He held out a hand to her. "I don't know all of what Dash said to you before, but I can tell you this much—not a day went by that we haven't thought about you. That night we kissed you, that wasn't a mistake. My only regret was that we never got another chance."

Her mouth quirked into a brief smile. "I thought Dash was supposed to be the smooth talker?"

"I must be rubbing off on him because I couldn't have said it any better, myself." Dash appeared at his side and held out his hand, too. "Please forgive us?"

"If I do, what then?" she asked.

"Then we finish what we started that night on the *Salan*. Like you said before, the war is over. There's nothing stopping us from spending time together. Getting to know each other," Mack said.

She stared at them both. "The way you've been acting, I thought you might hate me."

"Never." He'd felt a lot of things about Lieksa over the years, but hate wasn't one of them.

She scrubbed her hands on her thighs. "Why are you asking me out? I need you to be clear. I don't want to misunderstand what's going on."

Mack cleared his throat. "We want to take you out to dinner. Talk. Like I said, we want to get to know you and let you get to know us."

"You two want to date me? Not a hookup, but an actual date with dinner or something?" She sounded so wary it made his heart ache.

Dash chuckled. "Yeah, we do. Though I should warn you, we've never actually done that. We'll very likely screw up at least once more. Probably more than that."

She blinked. "You've never dated?"

"Never," Mack admitted. Sure, they had both dallied with women from time to time. They weren't monks. But there had only been one woman they wanted to be with for more than a night.

"No one else could compete with the memory of you. The others never stood a chance," Dash said, speaking for both of them.

For one painfully long moment, she didn't move or speak. Time stretched out until he was certain she was going to turn and walk away again. When she took a tentative step forward, he had to bite his tongue to avoid cheering aloud.

"One date, and we're going to talk. That's it, just talk. I want to hear about what happened after I left. How did you survive? What effect did the upgrade have on you both? How did you end up out here, working for another corporation? I have so many questions."

He and Dash moved together, taking her outstretched hand in theirs and drawing her in closer. "We'll tell you whatever you want to know. We've got questions, too. Where have you been? Why are you out here in the ass end of nowhere? Once Dash is cleared to get out of here, we're going out…somewhere."

She laughed, the sound making his heart feel like it was full of sunlight.

"Alright. As for Dash, he should be out of here by tomorrow."

"Then we're taking you out tomorrow night. A proper date." The more Mack thought about it, the more he liked this idea. If they were starting over, then this was the right way to do it.

"I suppose this means no kissing right now?" Dash grumbled.

"No kissing. We're starting over, remember?" she told him. "That's what we're doing, right? No more misunderstandings or accusations?"

"We're starting over," Mack agreed.

"How about one on credit?" Dash pressed.

"Nope. You still have a lot to make up for Dash Scudo. We all do." She tugged her hand out of their grasp. "I've got a couple more tests to run. The sooner they're done, the sooner he's out of here."

Mack took the hint. "That's my cue to go. I'll see you soon, Lieksa." He smiled at her then turned to his partner. "If she cuts you loose early, let me know and I'll meet you at home. I'm headed back to the office."

He brushed past her and was pleased when she didn't pull away from him. They had a long way to go yet, but it was a start.

CHAPTER FOUR

True to her word, Lieksa released him first thing in the morning, once the last of the test results were in. Dash alerted Mack to his new status as a free man and headed back to the residence they shared. Space was at a premium out here on the Drift, and every square inch of real estate came with a steep price tag. By combining their savings and their current income, they could afford far nicer living quarters than either of them could manage on their own.

He made his way to one of the banks of mag-lifts, waiting his turn before stepping into high-speed elevators that would deliver him to the upper levels of the station where he and Mack lived. On a normal day, he would have taken one of the bullet trains that crisscrossed the station, but after all the time he had been cooped up, he opted to walk. He needed to stretch his legs and get some fresh air. Well, as fresh as it got when one lived in a floating tin can on the edge of civilized space.

At least it didn't carry the lingering scents of antiseptic and sterilizers.

Unlike the main levels, where wide concourses were lined with countless bars, clubs, restaurants, and pharma dispensers, the residential levels were relatively quiet. The lighting in his sector was designed to mimic sunlight, and some well-intentioned but long departed administrator had decided to paint the ceiling sky-blue. The effect might have been pleasant once, but the paint was cracked and peeling away, marring the illusion with ragged holes and streaks of rust.

Exercise always helped clear his head, and right now, he needed that. Without a digital record, he was relying on his own memories, something he had never done before. His augmented abilities were a combination of behavioral programming and hardware. The human mind was an unreliable recording device at the best of times, so his creators simply conditioned him to ignore his own memories from the time he left his maturation tank.

Even after he had freed himself from his programming, Dash had never bothered to retrain himself to access his own memories. Why would he when he had a digital record of every important moment in his life? Every moment but the ones that had nearly been his last. It was time to change the way he did things. This gaping hole in his memory was something he never wanted to experience again.

He remembered gearing up for the raid and going over the plan for the hundredth time, orchestrating every second so that they knew exactly what would happen and where everyone would be from the moment they came through the doors. In the beginning, everything went smoothly. Mack was coordinating the attack from the rear, and Dash had been tasked with getting to high ground so he could see the entire area, then relay what he saw to Mack so he could adjust their plans on the fly.

Len took point, they had split off from the others, and that's where his recollection of events ended. There were fragments, but none of them made sense. A flash of a firearm discharging. A sense of confusion and...anger?

According to Len's report, they'd been fired on before they reached their planned vantage point. Dash had gone down first, and Len reported firing at the shooters before being hit himself.

"Damn it, why can't I remember?" The gaps in Dash's memory made him feel like a failure. Record and recall were part of his basic programming. More than that, they were the basis of his entire design. He and Mack were both highly specialized, created late in the war effort to fill specific niches. Unlike most cyborgs, he and Mack were created and trained individually. They weren't even batch siblings. They had bonded not only because of their compatible skills, but because they were treated as outsiders everywhere they went.

While the walk had him feeling better physically, he was still frustrated and struggling with his failures by the time he arrived home. His mood might have continued to darken, but Mack chose that moment to message him through their internal comm-channel.

"You home yet?" Mack asked.

"Walked through the door thirty seconds ago. What's up?"

"What the hell are we going to do with Lieksa tonight? It's fight night at the Nova Club." There was no mistaking the edge in his partner's tone. The unflappable Mack Darian was nervous.

Dash was grinning as he answered, grateful Mack couldn't see his expression. *"I think we can do better than blood sports and cheap beer for our angel. What about taking her to Amped?"*

Mack was quiet for a second. *"You think so?"*

"We want her to get to know us, right? Can you think of a better way? The food's good, the crowd's downright well-mannered by Drift standards, and we're guaranteed a table."

"I'll make a call and let them know we're dropping by."

"I'll figure out something to bring her. According to our married friends, gifts are important." Zura and Cynder would be able to point him in the right direction there.

"Good thinking. By the way, I'm only working a half-day. I've been ordered to take some down time before I burn out."

"Then I'll see you when you get home."

"That sounded alarmingly domesticated. Quit it."

Dash laughed as he best friend ended the conversation with his usual grumbling. The truth was, they had become domesticated over the past few years. They joined Corp-Sec right after they were released from service to the corporations. Unlike most of their fellow cyborgs, they hadn't drifted around the galaxy or tried to start lives anywhere else. They'd come to the Drift right away, learned the job, proved themselves to the doubters, and carved out a good life for themselves.

Tonight, they'd take Lieksa to their home away from home. Amped was one of the best live music bars on the station, and they spent a lot of time there. Sharing that part of their life with Lieksa was an important step in letting her get to know who they were and what they had achieved since the last time they were together.

He glanced at the time and groaned. He had a lot to do today, and not a lot of hours left to do it. The three of them had overcome enough challenges already. It would be nice if, just once this week, things went according to plan.

* * * *

"You're sure we're in the right place?" Mack asked Dash as they made their way through one of the rougher parts of Astek station.

"I'm sure. I'm not happy about it, but we are definitely in the right sector. It makes our part of the station seem downright luxurious, doesn't it?"

Mack snickered, but there wasn't much to laugh at. Their years in Corp-Sec gave them a deeper knowledge of the Drift than most of its residents would ever have. They knew every station and platform that made up the rag-tag community, but none better than the station where they lived and worked. "Why would she choose to live here?"

"No idea. It's not what I expected from a corporate lab-tech with her skills. This place is rough enough I'm regretting we're not armed." Dash glanced down a shadow-filled side-corridor, his nose wrinkling as an air vent blew a fetid blast of what should have been freshly recycled air at them.

"When did you turn into such a pansy? This is paradise compared to some of the battlefields we survived."

Dash pointed to the side of his head. The wound was gone, but they had shaved his hair around the injury, and it hadn't had time to grow back, yet.

"Getting shot in the head has reminded me that despite my god-like good looks and charm, I'm not actually immortal. I'm too pretty to die young, so I'm going to be more cautious from now on."

"My mistake, you've turned into a *paranoid* pansy. Lieksa walks through this sector every day, and she's still in one piece. I'll bet you the first round of drinks tonight that she doesn't even own a weapon."

"No bet. I can't see her ever wanting to hurt anyone."

Mack agreed, which was why he worried about her. Not just about where she lived, but her plans to help the doctor dig up information on what was done to Cynder and the others. It was too risky. They couldn't even bring it up with her without revealing that he and Dash had eavesdropped. Not their finest moment, but in their line of work, the rules were different. They couldn't make decisions without information, and obtaining intel was what he and Dash were designed to do.

They arrived at her door and activated the door chime, announcing their presence. Suddenly, he was nervous. His fist tightened around the flowers he held, and he had to remind himself not to crush the delicate blooms.

Dash's voice sounded in his head. *"Ready?"*

"No. What if we fraxx *this up?"*

"We won't. This is too important. We've been given a second chance. How often does that happen?"

The door made a low, grinding noise and slid open, and Mack's heart thundered in his chest as he stared at the vision in the doorway. She looked incredible.

The too-big outfits were gone, replaced by a dark green dress that skimmed her luscious curves. The dress left most of her shoulders bare, revealing the same tantalizing pattern of freckles he remembered from their one evening together. Her mane of red hair was free of its usual ponytail and tumbled over her shoulders in silken waves, and every breath he took was perfumed with the sugar-and-spice scent that had haunted his memories for years.

"Hello, angel," he managed to force a few words past his suddenly tight throat.

"Hi." She was smiling in welcome, but her shoulders were tight with tension, and she looked as if she might bolt from the doorway at any second.

"I'm really happy you're coming out with us tonight. And might I say, you look incredible. We're going to be the envy of every guy we meet with you on our arm," Dash said before switching to internal comms. *"Flowers, goofball. Give her the flowers."*

"These are for you," Mack held out the bouquet for her. Her smile brightened, and it felt like the whole damned room lit up when she did.

"Thank you."

She took the flowers, and when her fingers brushed over his, it was as if sparks showered across his skin. *Re'veth*, first he couldn't speak, and now he was hypersensitive. Either his implants were malfunctioning, or Lieksa's effect on him was stronger than ever.

"I'll just put these in water, if that's alright? You can come in if you like, but I should warn you, you'll probably fill most of the room." She moved away from the door and Mack followed her in.

She hadn't been kidding. Once Dash joined them, there wasn't much space left. Most of Astek station had been upgraded or revamped at one time or another, but apparently this sector had been overlooked. The living area was cramped and utilitarian, with every inch of space doing double or triple duty. The single bed doubled as a couch, the eating nook was also a workspace, and what little storage space there was would have to house everything from clothing to foodstuffs.

Lieksa lived a very minimal existence, even for someone who had spent years living on a hospital ship in deep space. There was nothing personal about the place at all. No art or mementos. In fact, the only personal item he could see was a picture of a large group of people that hung on the wall above her bed.

She busied herself in the small corner of the room that functioned as her kitchen. "You guys really didn't need to pick me up. I could've met you there."

"It was our pleasure, sweetheart. Besides, we'll have more time to talk this way. That's what this night is about, the three of us getting to know each other better."

She laughed at that. "I think you mean getting to know each other *at all*. Until I showed up at the med-center, you didn't even know my name."

Mack moved closer to her, which only required taking two steps to his left. "We might not have known your name, but we knew you. Your kindness. Your compassion, the way you bite your lower lip whenever you have to do something you're not sure about, like some of the tests they ordered you to do on us."

She spun around to face him, her eyes wide with surprise at finding him so close. "That's not what Dash said. He said what you did was a mistake you both regret."

"We already told you that wasn't true. I have a lot of regrets in my life, Lieksa Kiv, but kissing you isn't one of them. I do regret the way I've treated you since you came back into our lives. I regret that despite living on the same *fraxxing* space station, we didn't find each other until now. I'm sorry I doubted you. I shouldn't have, because I already know the most important thing about you. You're a kind, caring woman, and you deserved our trust."

"Thank you," she whispered. "That means a lot to me."

He gave in to temptation and reached out to cup her cheek. Her skin was as soft as he remembered, and her scent filled his senses, sending a surge of blood straight to his cock.

His heart might still have doubts, but that didn't stop him from wanting her. He'd felt this way from the first time he'd come to and found her standing at his bedside, humming softly to herself as she monitored his readouts on a half dozen machines.

For a moment, she tipped her head into his hand, accepting the contact, but all too soon she pulled away again.

From behind him, Dash spoke up. "Stealing those moments with you, showing you who we really were, that wasn't a mistake, Lieksa. I'm an idiot for ever saying such a thing. Tonight is about starting over. Somehow, we all ended up together again. I'd like to think that's fate's way of giving us a second chance."

She glanced past Mack to Dash and flashed him a brief smile before speaking. "Given how unlikely it was that we found each other again, I'll accept that maybe, this is supposed to happen. But one thing I've learned in my life is that when fate gives with one hand, it usually takes something with the other. The last time we were together, we all paid a steep price for it. I'm not sure I can do it again."

"How about we worry about prices and payments another day? I'm willing to risk that much, at least."

"So am I." Mack glanced at his watch. "And we should get going if we want to eat before the entertainment starts and it gets too loud to talk."

"Entertainment?" Lieksa queried. "What kind of entertainment?"

"Didn't he tell you where we're going?" Dash asked with a chuckle.

"No, he did not, and for that matter, neither did you," she said, arching a brow in challenge at them both.

"I thought it would be nice to surprise you, but since you're curious, we're going to a club called Amped. Heard of it?" he asked.

"Of course I have. I've never been there, though. It's not easy to get through the door unless you know someone, and I don't have many friends out here. How are we getting in? I thought there was a waitlist even to get a reservation."

He arched a brow back at her, enjoying this new, sharper edge she was showing. "As it happens, we know the owners. They've got a table set aside for us."

"Well, then, I guess we should go. I've heard the musicians are the best on the Drift. I miss live music. I used to go to concerts all the time when I lived on Earth. I'm not sure why I stopped."

Mack grinned. "I'm a fan of music, too. Something I got into after we were freed from service to the corporations."

Dash moved to the door and opened it before pausing to look back at them. "Coming?"

She glanced up at Mack with another shy smile. "I'd love to, but you're going to have to let me out of this corner, first."

He didn't even think about it, he acted on impulse. Instead of moving out of her way, he placed his hands on her waist and lifted her into the air before turning around so he was facing the door.

"Mack! I asked you to move, not to move me," she protested, but her hands were covering his, and she made no attempt to free herself.

He held her for a few more pleasurable seconds before setting her feet back on the ground. "My way was faster."

"Faster isn't always better."

"I was designed and trained to always take the fastest, most direct route to a solution."

She gave him an odd look. "Is that why you kissed me the first time? Because it was the most direct path to whatever problem you were trying to solve?"

"I kissed you because wanting you *was* the problem I intended to solve." He released her then, and she took a step backward, putting more distance between them.

Dash moved in behind her and took her hand. "Some things may have changed since we were last together, but there's one thing that's still the same. You're still our angel. Nothing we've been through has changed that for us, and I'm starting to believe nothing ever could."

"But you've both been so angry with me."

"What can I say? We're complicated guys. Come with us, sweetheart. The rest of this conversation is going to require something you don't have enough of here," Dash said.

"What's that, space?"

"Nope." Mack pointed to the door. "Liquor."

They left her tiny residence and started walking, keeping Lieksa safely tucked between them. They walked slower than usual, because despite her being tall for a woman, her strides were still shorter than both of theirs. As they made the short walk back to the central bank of mag-lifts for this sector, Mack noticed Lieksa's hand was still in Dash's. He reached down and took her free hand. She glanced up at him in surprise but didn't pull away.

Score one for team cyborg.

CHAPTER FIVE

It was strange to walk past the lineup of hopeful patrons waiting to enter Amped. More than a few envious and resentful looks were shot their way as the security guard at the door greeted her dates by name and welcomed them inside, bypassing the line completely.

"Come here often, do you?" she asked as they went inside.

"As often as we can. Depending on what we feel like doing, we're usually here or at the Nova Club," Dash said, raising his voice to be heard over the music and noise that filled the air.

"Never been there either. Isn't that kind of a rough crowd?"

"Depends on the night. Fight nights, sure. But the owners are friends and fellow veterans of the Resource Wars." Mack glanced down at her. "You've been here more than a year, I would've thought you'd seen more of the station by now."

What could she say to that without sounding utterly pathetic? She didn't go out much because she had no friends on the station, and going out alone wasn't something she enjoyed. "I always meant to explore more, but somehow I never got around to it."

Mack smiled at her, and her brain melted a little around the edges. When he looked at her like that, it was hard to remember any of the reasons she was trying to keep some distance between them. She wanted to feel their hands on her skin again, to be caught between them in a heated tangle of kisses and caresses until the world went away and took all her doubts and worries with it.

Dash turned to look at her, his smile as warm and inviting as Mack's. "We know every inch of this station, and a good portion of the rest of the Drift. If you want to go exploring sometime, sweetheart, we'd be happy to play tour guide."

"I think I'd like that," she said as her heart did a little skippity-hop. They weren't even sitting down to dinner yet, and her body was already betraying her. Her heart still ached from their accusations, but she wanted to forgive them. *Veth*, she wanted it so much it scared her.

Everything about them scared her. Last time they'd been together it had been a brief encounter, a promise of things none of them believed would ever come because there were too many barriers. This time, they had a chance at something real, and she wasn't sure she was ready for that.

She wasn't sure she deserved it.

After what she had done to the cyborgs assigned to her, the testing and experiments she'd done, did she even have the right to be happy?

"You're chewing on your lip again. What's bothering you?" Mack asked.

She blew out a breath and forced herself to let go of her worries for the moment. "Just nervous," she said, which was true enough.

To her surprise, Mack chuckled, then lowered his voice to a conspirator's whisper. "Me too, angel. Glad to know I'm not alone."

His confession helped her relax and get out of her head. She smiled back and finally looked around and got her first real impressions of the bar. It was crowded, which she had expected, but despite the number of patrons, there was space between the tables, leaving the serving staff plenty of room to maneuver.

There was an old-fashioned feeling to the place, and it took her a while to figure out why. It wasn't just one or two details that inspired the sense of nostalgia, it was a combination of dozens of thoughtful touches. The walls appeared to be made of dark wood paneling, which was unlikely given the incredible cost of shipping wood out to the far reaches of the galaxy. The chairs were designed for comfort, with high backs and deep cushions upholstered in rich shades of red and gold. The walls were covered in black and white photographs of musicians, some posing, others performing.

It was a comfortable, welcoming place, and she regretted that she hadn't put more effort into coming here before now. It was exactly the kind of place she used to enjoy when she lived on Earth.

Dash led the way through the crowd, working his way to a raised platform not far from the stage where the performers would be playing later tonight. He nodded to the bouncer guarding the stairs leading to the platform and walked right past him.

"Um, are we supposed to be up there?" she asked.

Mack slipped an arm around her waist and grinned. "We most certainly are. Welcome to the VIP section."

He guided her to a curved booth with a perfect view of the stage. A light cube set on the table cast a small amount of illumination that slowly shifted colors from red to gold and back again. It provided enough light to see, while leaving enough shadow to give an illusion of privacy.

"How did you guys manage to get VIP seating? Is this a Corp-Sec perk?" she asked, gesturing around them to the empty section.

"Nope. This is because we're awesome," Dash replied with a wink.

"Like we mentioned, we know the owners. You'll meet T'arv and his mate, Nadia later. They're going to want to meet you."

"Me? Why?"

Mack turned and gave her lopsided smile. "Because in all the years we've been coming here, we've never brought a date. They're going to know you're special simply because you're here with us."

She exhaled sharply. "In that case, I vote we start on the drinks right away."

"Good thinking." Dash raised a hand, and a server appeared out of the shadows.

"Good evening, Mr. Scudo and Mr. Darian. It's nice to see you again. Will you be having your usual?"

"Hi, Jinella. How's the family? Is your boy still determined to join the IAF and become a pilot some day?"

The woman laughed and shook her head. "He's decided that Interstellar Armed Forces officers have to get up too early. Now he's all about long-haul freight hauling. He figures that gives him more time to sleep and goof off."

"He might be onto something there. As for us, I think we'll start with a bottle of champagne. Ask Nadia to pick out something nice for us."

Jinella smiled. "Celebrating?"

Mack reached over and took Lieksa's hand. "Yes, we are."

Lieksa didn't say a word until they were alone again. "Aren't we supposed to be talking?"

"Can't we do both? We're all here. That fact alone is worth celebrating. We thought we'd lost each other, and you came back at the right moment to put Dash back together."

She couldn't argue with his reasons. Not that she wanted to.

Jinella soon returned with a bottle and several champagne flutes, pouring each of them a glass before setting the bottle down in the center of the table. "Nadia recommends this one, and asked if you'd like her to create a special meal to go with it."

Dash grinned. "If our lovely hostess would like to create a meal for us, then I'm certainly not going to argue. Sweetheart, would that be okay with you?"

"That sounds lovely," she said, surprised by the offer. "You must be quite good friends with the owners," she observed.

Dash and Mack looked at each other for moment, and she somehow knew they were communicating via their internal channel. Within a few seconds, Mack tightened his fingers around hers, and Dash cleared his throat.

"We met them the first night this place opened. We dropped by after our shift ended to check the place out and wound up talking with Nadia and T'arv until long after closing time. We've been coming here ever since."

"And being among their first customers garners you this kind of special treatment?" She gestured around them.

"Occasionally I make Mack sing for his supper. It's a fair trade, I think."

Lieksa had been distracted enough by the conversation to miss the slender male Pheran approaching until he appeared beside their booth. His large silver eyes gleamed with good-natured amusement. His variegated blue skin tone made him hard to see in the dim light of the bar, but she could tell he was tall and lithe, with vaguely feline features, including a pair of tufted ears.

"T'arv! It's good to see you. I thought you'd be too busy setting up for tonight to come visit with us." Mack greeted his friend with a smile. "I'd like you to meet someone. T'arv Anas, this is Lieksa Kiv. Lieksa, this is T'arv, one of the galaxy's greatest music lovers."

"It's nice to meet you." She turned to stare at Mack. "You *sing*?"

"And plays the guitar. He's the best student I've ever had. It's good to see these two out with someone for once. When I heard they weren't alone, I had to come see for myself."

"It's just a drink," she said, but her cheeks heated as T'arv only grinned wider in response. "I still can't believe you sing, Mack. Dash, are you a secret drummer or something?"

"There's not a musical bone in this sexy body. I'll share my passions with you some other time, angel."

Lieksa shivered as the sensual undertone of Dash's words flowed over her like a silken caress. Her body responded as if he'd actually touched her; pulse racing, skin feverishly hot, her pussy suddenly slick with need.

"Angel?" T'arv's brows raised in surprise. "Not *the* angel?"

Mack nodded. "The one and only."

T'arv looked about ready to burst with questions, but Mack cut him off with a slash of his hand.

"We'll tell you all about it another time. Tonight, we're celebrating."

"You have more to celebrate than I thought. Dash, it's good to see you back on your feet. I hear we nearly lost you." T'arv absently tugged on a lock of his blue-black hair before continuing. "I was going to ask a favor of you, Mack, but since you're celebrating…"

"I'm not here to sing, T'arv. Not tonight."

"Why not?" Lieksa asked. "I'd like to hear you perform. I mean, if you want to."

"You would?" Mack asked. "You sure?"

"I'm sure." She forced a note of confidence into her response. It was insane that she could be utterly sure of herself when it came to her job and abilities, and useless when it came to taking control of the rest of her life.

"Wonderful! Two songs is all I need from you, Mack, and you can return to your date." T'arv winked at Lieksa. "I wouldn't dream of keeping you away from this lovely lady for long. Enjoy your evening."

When he was gone, Dash raised his glass. "I think we should start this night off right. A toast. To finding each other again."

They touched glasses and drank. Lieksa took several sips of hers. She was going to need a little liquid courage to get through the night.

Dash set his drink down on the table and turned to look at her. The time had come for answers. The sooner they had this part out of the way, the sooner they could move on with their lives. "Alright, sweetheart. This is the part where you tell us why you ran."

"It was the only way to save you. The upgrade worked *too* well. My superiors would have wanted to run tests to find out why, and when they did, they would have realized you had defeated your behavior programming and become entirely self-aware. I filed a false report stating the experiment was a total failure and shouldn't be repeated. I made sure you were transferred off the hospital ship and back to combat before anyone could double check my findings. Then I resigned and took the first transport out."

"Why didn't you tell us what you were doing?" Mack asked.

"I couldn't. It wasn't like I could send you a message, and if I saw you again..." she shook her head and sighed. "I knew if I saw either of you again, I'd be tempted to do something foolish. It was too risky. There hasn't been a day since then that I haven't thought about the two of you. When the war ended, I did what I could to help the other cyborgs gain their freedom. If Astek ever finds out what I did, I'd be fired so fast I'd hit light speed on my way out the door."

"Your secret is safe with us." Dash gave in to the need that had been pushing him since the first time he'd seen her again. He tangled a hand into the thick fall of her hair and drew her in close. When she didn't pull away, he leaned in and brushed a delicate kiss to her lips. He only intended to kiss her once, but all his good intentions vaporized the moment his mouth met hers. He'd been waiting for this moment for years, reliving their brief time together time and again in his memories. They were nothing compared to the reality of having her back in his arms again.

Her lips were warm and tasted of champagne, and her hair was the same silken weight he'd caressed a thousand times in his dreams.

"Does this mean I'm forgiven?" she asked between kisses.

"I'm pretty sure there's nothing to forgive. You did what you thought you had to. You were trying to protect us. I just wish you could have found a way to tell us what you were doing. *Fraxx*, it would have been nice to know your real name."

She laughed and for the first time, leaned in to kiss him, branding his mouth with hers for several slow, delicious moments before answering him.

"It never occurred to me you didn't know it, but how could you have?"

She took her hand, running her fingertips over the barcode imprinted on the inside of his left wrist. Every cyborg in existence carried that same mark, a permanent reminder of a time when they were thought of as commodities instead of living beings. "I don't know how I missed the signs. I worked with cyborgs every day. How could I have been so blind?"

"You weren't blind. Even when you didn't know the truth, you treated us with kindness and compassion," Mack said, moving in close enough to be able to nuzzle Lieksa's hair. "That's what I first noticed about you. You *cared* about us. How was I supposed to stay away from you once I realized that?"

"Red hair, a kind heart, and a gentle touch. We were doomed right from the start." Dash turned his hand over and captured hers in his fist.

"Afterward...I swore I'd never work on another cyborg or anything that could possibly be sentient. After everything I did to you, how can you forgive me so easily? I've never forgiven myself."

"You saved our lives the first time we met. More than once, it turns out. The second time we crossed paths, you saved mine yet again. I think that's grounds for a little forgiveness and understanding. If we couldn't do that, do you think we'd be working for a corporation like Astek?"

"I wondered about that. At first, I thought it was the only work you could find. But Alyson told me you two have been here since the Drift was first set up. You really don't mind working for the corporations after all they did to cyborgs?"

"After the Resource War ended and the spoils had been divvied up, there weren't many jobs left that didn't involve some sort of corporate connection. Most of the freighters, mining ships, and stations in the galaxy either work for them directly or depend on them for their livelihood. Our choices were simple. Sign on for more fighting with the IAF, work for the corporations, or go live in a backwater colony somewhere and try to eke out a living as a farmer." Mack snickered. "Do you see either of us as the farming type?"

Her musical laughter was a song Dash's heart wanted to dance to.

She was still laughing when their meal arrived. All conversation faded to appreciative silence as Jinella and another server set out the feast Nadia had arranged for them.

"I haven't met Nadia yet, but I think she's already my new favorite friend," Lieksa declared with a grin.

"She's an amazing cook. Great voice, too. In fact, she's almost perfect."

"Yeah, apart from that one flaw of hers," Mack muttered and glanced around as if he was expecting Nadia to appear at any second.

"What flaw is that?" Lieksa asked.

"She's a hugger," Dash whispered with a theatrical shudder.

"And that's a flaw?"

"A big one," Mack chimed in.

Lieksa nearly choked on the first mouthful of her dinner. "Big, scary, cyborg soldiers turned Corp-Sec officers should not be afraid of hugs."

"We're not the touchy-feely type," Mack said.

She set down her fork and looked first at Mac, then at Dash. "Really? Because I don't recall you two ever having trouble getting touchy or feely with me."

"You're the exception to the rule."

"You're the exception to all our rules, sweetheart." It was the truth. Since the day they'd woken up and found themselves under her care, she'd affected them in ways no other woman had. Dash didn't understand it. He didn't need to.

CHAPTER SIX

Lieksa couldn't remember the last time she had been out enjoying herself like this. Mack and Dash focused all their attention on her, engaging her with questions and stealing the occasional kiss as they ate, drank, and talked. They told her stories about Corp-Sec and how the Drift had slowly evolved into a community over the years, and she filled them in on the jobs she'd held and the places she had visited since resigning from Nobar Tech.

They particularly liked hearing stories about her time on a passenger liner that made a continuous circuit between Earth and the Pheran star system. Officially, her job was to repair and maintain the numerous robots that catered to the every need and whim of the passengers. The reality was that she spent most of her time rebuilding child-tending models torn apart by their spoiled charges and making repairs to overworked sex-bots. Three months of that was more than enough for her. That led to a short stint on a freighter headed to the Drift. The moment she stepped foot on Astek station, she knew it was the right place for her.

It felt like no time at all before T'arv appeared again, this time carrying a guitar case which he set down on the recently cleared table.

"I juggled the schedule a bit so you're up first, Mack. I really appreciate you doing this for me. Nadia nearly had my ears when she heard I'd asked you to sing tonight. My beloved *vardi* accused me of having no romance in my soul. Me! She sends apologies by the way. She's been trying to get out to say hello, but we're short-staffed tonight, and the kitchen's a bit of a madhouse. Not that I'd say that to her face, or she really would have my ears," T'arv said, wiggling his tufted blue ears for emphasis.

"Tell your *vardi* that I asked him to sing for me. I've never been serenaded before."

T'arv grinned and winked at her. "I'll do that." He rapped his knuckles on the table and turned to go. "Backstage in five minutes, Mack."

"I'll be there."

"Are you going to tell me which songs you're going to sing, or is it a surprise?" she asked him.

"You wouldn't know the song even if I told you the title. This club is the only place it's ever been performed." Mack leaned in and kissed her before she could ask him anything more about it.

Where Dash's first kiss had been gentle and coaxing, Mack's was a sensual assault.

His lips slanted over hers, sending shockwaves of pure desire tearing through her body.

"I should have kissed you the first second you came back to us. I'm sorry I waited so long."

"You were hurt and angry, not to mention the fact Dash had gone and gotten himself shot again."

"Yeah, there was that," Mack murmured before kissing her again.

"I'm going to develop a complex if you two keep this up. I do not get shot that often. Three, no, four times in a lifetime is not that many. And the first time we met, it was because *both* of us got shot, remember?"

"The only reason I was injured was because I was carrying your wounded ass at the time."

Dash spluttered and started to argue, but Mack cut him off with a wave of his hand. "You can defend your honor later, I'm due backstage."

"Don't *fraxx* up, my friend."

"I'll do my best not to."

She didn't care if he screwed up or not, he was going to sing for her.

"I'll see you soon, angel," he said to her. Grabbing the guitar case as he got to his feet, he headed in the same direction T'arv had gone.

"He never forgot about you. Neither of us did. And if it took getting shot again to bring you back into our lives, then I'm glad I never learned to duck."

"Do you remember anything yet? I think the data is still encoded in your hardware, but I'm not sure how to retrieve it. Whoever shot you couldn't have picked a better spot to aim for. If it had been any other cyborg, they would have died. The only thing that saved you was the upgrade I gave you the first time you were in my care."

He absently touched the spot behind his ear where he'd been injured. "It's all still a blank. I hate not being able to remember anything."

"I can imagine. You're not having any trouble remembering things since the injury, though? Your memory and digital recall are working fine?"

"They are. I'm going to be able to remember this night perfectly."

She blushed but ignored the blatant flirtation. "I'll keep working on the problem. And you might still remember something about the attack on your own. Give yourself time to heal and recalibrate. The mind is an amazingly resilient thing."

"You are utterly irresistible when you're like this," he declared and wrapped an arm around her shoulders, tucking her in against his side.

Their bodies were in contact from thigh to shoulder, and she was aware of every hard, muscled inch of him. "When I'm like what?" she managed to get the words out despite the distraction of having him so close.

"Like this. Concerned and wanting to take care of me. You get this little furrow between your brows, and your voice goes soft. You're the only woman in the worlds who has ever looked at me that way. Like I matter."

"Of course you matter! You're a ranking officer in Corp-Sec. You're part of the community here."

"That's not what I meant. You've *always* looked at me that way, sweetheart. Even when you didn't know the truth about what we were, you still cared. You've got the kindest heart of anyone I've ever known."

Her cheeks burned, and she looked down at her hands.

"I'm glad you found your way back to us. You need someone to tell you how special you are. Judging by the way you're blushing right now, you don't hear it often enough."

She lifted her head to deny it, and he sealed her mouth with a kiss that blasted away every argument she had. His tongue stroked hers, lips mated, breath mingled. Before she could think about it, she had her hands in his hair, pulling him closer.

He groaned her name, and she whispered his back. Then, there was no need for words. One kiss led to another, then another. She lost track of the world around them until Dash lifted his head with a rueful chuckle. "If you miss Mack's performance, he's going to be royally pissed at me."

Sure enough, the lights had dimmed, and the stage was now lit, though no one was on it, yet. "He's really going up there?"

"He really is. Music is his passion. Has been since the first time T'arv handed him a guitar. It's the one thing that's all his, you know?"

She nodded, even though she didn't truly understand. How could she? She had a family. A childhood. No one had ever treated her the way the cyborgs had been treated.

T'arv walked onto the stage and walked up beside the single stool that sat in the center of it. "As always, I want to thank you all for coming tonight. Now, it's been a while since he's been up here, but I know you all know our first performer, so give him a big round of applause and welcome him back to the stage. Mack Darian's singing for us tonight!"

The applause and cheers were louder than she expected. Mack apparently had a fan following. She also didn't expect him to walk out on stage wearing a completely different outfit than he had worn at dinner. The black slacks and charcoal top were gone, replaced by black denim pants that fit sinfully well, and a blue silk shirt beneath a black leather jacket. It was an old fashioned look, but he made it work.

He sat on the stool and settled the guitar he carried into his lap, running a hand over the strings before looking out at the audience. "Good evening everyone, and welcome to Amped."

Sound amplifiers carried his voice to every part of the bar, and there was another round of cheers in response to his welcome. When it was quiet again, he strummed another chord and then looked straight at her. "Tonight, I'm going to sing a personal favorite of mine. This one's for you, Lieksa. It's always been for you."

Her heart pounded in her chest, and a thrill chased down her spine as he started to play.

A long time ago
For one brief, shining moment
I had everything I dreamed of
In the palm of my hand

But dreams don't last forever
And loss is part of living
I'd give up all my tomorrows
To go back to yesterday

She was my heaven-sent angel
With a heart made for caring
A soul as gentle as her touch
And starlight in her eyes,

She left and took my heart with her
Now my universe is darker.
Her star's gone out, but I know,
She's forever in my heart.

"Hey, no tears," Dash whispered as Mack continued to sing. He wiped away the tears she wasn't even aware were falling.

"But, it's about me. Isn't it?" She knew the answer already. Mack wasn't only a singer, he was a songwriter, and he'd written this song about her.

"I told you, angel. He never forgot about you."

Mack reached the chorus again, and the last words were enough to make her tear up all over again. It was the most amazing, beautiful thing anyone had ever done for her.

Before she could say anything, Mack started to play again. It was an upbeat song, and vaguely familiar. She was still trying to figure out where she knew it from when Dash rose from the table, grabbed her by the hand, and pulled her up into his arms.

"Dance with me."

"I can't dance," she protested quietly.

"No one's looking at us. All you have to do is hold onto me and move to the music."

He swept her around, guiding her across the shadowed floor with surprising skill.

"Where did you learn to dance? I know that wasn't something you picked up during the war."

"There wasn't much to do on the trip out here but watch vids, read, and spend time in the sim pods. One of the sim programs was an introduction to dancing. It was more fun than playing cards with Mack. He can't bluff to save his life."

"Good to know. If I want an honest answer, I'll make sure to ask Mack."

He slid a hand down her spine, drawing her in close enough she could feel the hard line of his cock pressed against her. "I'll never lie to you. If you ask me a question, I'll tell you the truth about anything you want to know."

"I won't lie to you either. I'm tired of secrets."

His head bowed so that he could whisper his next words in her ear. "Thank you for keeping ours. I'm sorry it cost you so much."

"It was worth it," she whispered back.

By the time the song ended she was breathless and giddy with laughter and the effects of the champagne. Dash gave her one last twirl and escorted her back to their table. She watched Mack take a bow, wondering how long it would be until he rejoined them. She wanted to tell him how much his song had meant to her. This entire evening had turned into something so special, she would remember it for the rest of her life.

Mack usually enjoyed his moment in the spotlight, but tonight he couldn't wait to get off the stage and back to Lieksa. He jumped off the stage with the guitar still in his hand and headed straight for the VIP section.

Lieksa met him on the stairs, her face alight with happiness. *Veth*, she was beautiful.

"You were amazing!" she declared and threw her arms around him.

The joy of hearing her approval was eclipsed by the pleasure of having her back in his arms, this time of her own volition. "You liked it?"

"I loved it. The lyrics, your playing, the way you sing, all of it."

"Thank you. When I wrote that song, I never imagined I'd get to play it for you one day."

"It was beautiful. You made *me* sound beautiful. I know it was just a song, but thank you."

"You are so beautiful. And you're welcome." He was out of words, so he simply kissed her until she melted against him with a sweet little moan that fired his blood and had his dick harder than hull-plating in a matter of seconds.

"If you drop T'arv's guitar he's going to be pissed at you," Dash said via their internal channel.

He had a point. Not to mention the middle of Amped wasn't exactly the most private spot for a seduction. Not that he was going to seduce her. That wasn't the plan. Tonight was about getting to know each other, not getting her naked.

"Dash is getting jealous," he told her after stealing one last kiss.

"There's no chance he'd admit any such thing, but if you think we should head back to the table, I'm in agreement. Between dancing with Dash and kissing you, I've made enough of a spectacle of myself for one evening."

He guided her back to where Dash was waiting for them. He'd refilled their glasses with the last of their second bottle of champagne while he was waiting.

"You sounded good tonight, Mack. Maybe you should borrow T'arv's guitar more often," Dash said by way of greeting.

"Are you wearing T'arv's clothes too? Where did you get the new outfit?" Lieksa ran a finger along the sleeve of his leather jacket, and he idly wished she was touching his skin, instead.

"I keep a few changes of clothes in the back. We both do. That way we can come here after a shift and not have to worry about going home first, or sitting around in our uniforms all night."

"This place really is like your second home, isn't it?"

Dash's voice sounded in his head. *"Let's tell her."*

"Why?"

"Because I promised her there wouldn't be any more secrets."

"In our line of work, there will always be secrets," he reminded Dash. *"But yeah, we should tell her."*

"It's a little more than that, actually. We're T'arv's silent partners. Amped is half ours." Dash grinned at her. "Surprise."

"You own half this place? But, how? I mean, it's one of the biggest draws on the station!"

"It wasn't always a big draw. T'arv and Nadia had the know-how to make this place work, but there weren't many customers early on."

Dash snorted with laughter. "There weren't that many potential customers on the whole *fraxxing* station back then. They needed cash flow, and we had the scrip the corporations owed us in back pay, so we invested. You're the only one who knows outside of the four partners."

She looked around the crowded bar with a dazed expression on her face. "If this is half yours, then why do you two work at all?"

"When we were freed, Dash and I spent a lot of time talking about what we wanted to do with our lives. Drifting around, looking for a home wasn't something that appealed to me. I wanted a purpose, a goal."

"For the record, I was suggested an intergalactic pub crawl while we figured out what we wanted to be when we grew up," Dash said, then raised his glass to Mack. "I still think we should have done that, ya killjoy."

Lieksa giggled. "You bought half a bar instead. All the booze, none of the boring space travel. I think you made the right call."

"It didn't take long for her to get you figured out, did it?"

Dash shrugged and took a drink before answering. "I'm not the complicated one in this friendship. Complicated and broody are your domains."

"I'm not broody, I'm thoughtful. There's a difference."

"So, you work because you want to. And you chose Corp-Sec."

He nodded. "We wanted to do something that made a difference. I know it's a cliché, but to protect and serve is a noble purpose. After the war, we needed to do something good."

"We spent most of our time skulking in the shadows, gathering data. I'd trick   people into giving away information, relay it to Mack for analysis, and then we'd end up running like hell when they eventually figured out I wasn't supposed to be there. Fun times."

"That was something I always wondered about. I know you were programmed to act more human than most cyborgs, but how did you hide the barcode?"

Dash held out his hand so that the barcode on his inner wrist showed. "Like this."

The barcode faded away, leaving his wrist bare. There was a time Mack had envied that ability. Dash had enjoyed a freedom few cyborgs dreamed of during the wars. He could slip off the collar and be completely human for a few hours now and then.

"You shouldn't be able to do that." Lieksa was staring at Dash's wrist with fascination.

"My designers violated quite a few regulations when they created me. I was a spy, remember? Blending in was necessary, and to do that, they ignored, bent, or flat out broke the rules governing cyborg development and behavior."

"I heard whispers, but none of us knew anything for sure. How long does it last?"

"One hundred and eighty minutes. That's the maximum anyone felt comfortable letting me pretend to be human."

She reached for their hands, gripping them tight. "I'm glad neither of you has to pretend to be someone you're not anymore. When I thought you were dead, it always haunted me that you never got a chance to live a real life. I'm happy you're getting that chance, now."

"We got that chance in part because of you," Mack reminded her. It was something he would never let her, or himself, forget again.

CHAPTER SEVEN

Nadia had delivered dessert in person, setting down a tray filled with bite-sized versions of their most popular confections before beaming at Lieksa and introducing herself. Dash half expected her to explode with happiness. Nadia had fussed and clucked at them for years to find a nice girl, and it was clear by the way she was looking at Lieksa that she had the older woman's approval. Nadia and T'arv were the closest thing to parents he and Mack had ever known, and it pleased him no end to be able to introduce Lieksa to them both.

It was late by the time they left the bar, but none of them were ready to end the date, yet. They wandered the main concourse of the station with no real destination in mind for almost an hour before finally making their way back to Lieksa's residence cubby. It wasn't any better the second time he saw it.

"Have you ever considered living in another part of the station?" Mack asked, as direct as ever.

"Not really. I know it's not the nicest area, but rent is cheap." She shrugged slightly. "And to be honest, it reminds me of home."

"*This* reminds you of *Earth*?" Dash asked, gesturing to the deteriorating walls and dank shadows.

"A little, yeah. Have you ever been there, or have you just seen vids and sims?" she asked.

"Never been there."

"Not the most welcoming place for cyborgs," Mack added.

"It's not like the vids. Blue sky and lush green spaces, shining cities of glass and steel. Those exist, sure, but most people live in hive cities. Huge, self-contained superstructures crammed full of people living in cubbies a lot like the one I'm in. That's the world I knew. My family didn't have a lot of money. Too many mouths to feed, clothe, and educate."

"You're from a big family? I didn't know that, sweetheart."

"I'm the oldest of five kids." She hesitated for a second before adding. "My parents are in a triad, my mom, and my two dads. That's not as accepted on Earth as it is out here, so I don't talk about it much."

"Well, that explains why you didn't freak out the first time we both kissed you. I confess I wondered about that."

She laughed and glanced up at him. "You know, it never occurred to me to freak out over that. I was too busy trying to process the fact Mack wasn't obeying orders and both of you were secretly human to worry about anything else."

Mack stopped in the middle of the corridor and turned to face her. "It doesn't bother you, does it? Dating both of us?"

"Of course not. If it did, I wouldn't have spent tonight holding your hands and kissing you both," she pointed out. "If we're doing this, then I assume we're doing this together, the three of us."

"That's the plan. Does this mean we're going to be going out for a second date?"

She tipped her head to one side and tapped a finger to her lips. The motion sent her hair spilling over her shoulder in a fiery cascade, tempting Dash to wrap it around his fist and pull her in for another kiss.

"If I say yes, what are you going to come up with to top tonight? You've set the bar pretty high," she said.

Mack chuckled. "I'm glad to hear it. Next time, I want to dance with you, too."

"I'd like that. So, I guess that means we're going out again."

"Yes, we are. Soon." By the time they reached her door, Dash had a plan...of sorts. Mack would no doubt argue it was barely a concept, which was why he had no intention of sharing his plan until it was already in motion.

"Good night, sweetheart," he pulled Lieksa into his arms and kissed her. *Veth*, he was never going to get tired of having her in his arms again.

She kissed him back, her arms twining around his neck and her soft body rubbing up against his in ways that had him hard, hot, and aching with need.

Mack moved in behind her, pressing her between them. She turned to kiss Mack without letting go of Dash, and it was the most erotic thing he'd ever experienced.

By the time she wished them good night and vanished into her cubby, all of them were breathless, rumpled, and aroused.

Mack ran a hand through his hair and groaned. "I know we agreed that tonight was about reconnecting, but *fraxx*, I'm starting to question that choice right now."

"Glad to hear it, because I'm about to put my brilliant plan into action." He pulled out his comm and called Lieksa. All she had to do was say yes.

* * * *

Lieksa felt like she was dancing on air. The door slid shut behind her with its usual grinding sound. She floated over to her kitchenette and buried her face in the flowers they had given her earlier. Their delicate perfume had filled the small space while she was out, and their vibrant red, orange, and yellow petals added a splash of color to her otherwise dull quarters.

Her happy mood was curbed by the incessant chime of her comm. There was only one person who could be calling this late. Zale. No doubt he wanted to know if she would come into work tomorrow, despite it being her day off. She hadn't set foot in her workshop yet, and the work would be piling up. She didn't even bother checking the incoming ID before answering. "Hi, Zale. No, I'm not coming into work tomorrow, and there's nothing you can say to change my mind."

"Does this mean you're free tomorrow?"

"Dash? Yes, I have tomorrow free. I've been taking care of a certain cyborg for the last few days, and I've earned some time off."

"The way I figure it, we said good night, and you closed the door. That means our first date is officially over. So…. Want to go out on our second date?"

"Now?" Her heart did a triple flip in her chest at the idea of seeing them again.

"Right now. Say yes, angel. We're not ready for this night to end."

There were probably a dozen good, valid reasons why she should say no, but at the moment she couldn't think of a single one. "Yes."

She could hear Dash cheering from the other side of the door and grinned. It was nice to know she wasn't the only one losing her mind.

"Where are we going?" she asked, turning back to the door to open it for them.

She expected Dash to be standing there, but it was Mack's big frame that filled the doorway.

"That depends," he said, stepping inside and pulling her in close. "We can go anywhere on the station you want, or if you'd prefer, we can stay right here."

"My bed's not big enough for all three of us," she said, then slammed a hand over her mouth. "I—I mean my *place* isn't big enough for us. Not—I didn't mean—"

Mack cut off her mortified babbling with a scorching kiss while Dash laughed in the background.

"Sweetheart, I think I speak for both of us when I say we're really hoping you *did* mean what you said the first time."

Mack lifted his head so that their mouths were a scant inch apart and stared into her eyes. "Did you mean it?"

She nodded, not trusting herself to speak in case she started to babble again.

He caught her chin in his hand and tipped her head back so that she was looking into his eyes. She was fascinated with the way they changed color depending on his mood. Right now they were a vivid green and gold, the brown shades lost to the fires of desire that burned in his gaze.

"You have to say the words. Say you meant it," he told her in a low rumbling tone with a hint of command to it. It reminded her of the first night when he had refused her order and kissed her instead of letting her go.

"I meant what I said the first time."

"Do you want us to take you to bed?" Mack prompted.

"A bigger bed than the one here?" Dash added.

Her cheeks felt like were on fire, but she managed to get the words out. "Yes, please."

"Anything you want, angel. All you ever have to do is ask, and we'll try our damnedest to make it happen." Mack rubbed the pad of his thumb over her lower lip, released her, and stepped back.

Dash moved in to take his place, his stormy blue eyes dancing with gleeful satisfaction as he swooped in and kissed her. He buried his hands in her hair, holding her in place as his mouth slanted across hers. His kisses were hot and hungry, his touch firm but insistent, keeping control of her as he took the kiss deeper. He didn't relent until her knees threatened to buckle and the room was spinning.

"Thank you for saying yes," he whispered when he finally lifted his head to smile down at her.

"After that kiss, I'm pretty sure I should be the one thanking you," she said, holding tight to his shirt as she struggled to catch her breath.

He chuckled. "You say the nicest things, sweetheart. Do you want to pack a bag before we go?"

She blushed again and nodded. "I should."

"Don't take long."

She managed not to laugh. It wouldn't take her long to pack even if she took everything she owned. She lived simply and sent what little scrip she saved back to her family on Earth. They needed it more than she did. She squeezed past Mack and pulled open one of the storage panels that lined the walls. It didn't take long to find a bag and fill it with a change of clothes and a few other items. She wanted to be on her way before she started second guessing herself.

"Ready," she announced.

"Then let's go home." Mack took the bag from her and slung it over his shoulder. She followed them out, and for the second time that night she was certain her feet weren't even touching the floor.

* * * *

By the time they got home, Mack was close to his breaking point. Every step ratcheted up his anticipation, and he knew he wasn't alone. The three of them were sitting on a powder keg, and it would only take a spark to set them off. Once that happened, there would be no turning back, no changing trajectory. He didn't have enough data to know where they were headed, and for once, he didn't care about the outcome.

"You two are full of surprises," she said as they arrived at their home.

"How so?" Dash asked.

"Your lives have changed so much." She glanced up at them, and Mack saw a flicker of doubt in her ice-blue eyes. "Are you sure you want this? I don't really fit into your world anymore."

"Are we sure? *Re'veth*, woman. I've never been so sure of anything in my life," Dash said, echoing Mack's thoughts of only a moment before.

"Somehow, against all the odds, the three of us are together again." Mack pulled her into his arms and leaned in close. He needed her to hear his words and understand. "I have no idea how this is going to play out. All I know is that after years of dreaming about you and wondering what might have been, we've got you back. Second chances don't come around very often, and I'm not letting this one pass us by."

Her soft mouth turned up into a smile. "Neither am I."

He lifted her into his arms and walked through the door Dash had opened a second before. Once inside, he spun her around and pinned her to the nearest wall. His control shredded like Keski silk in a plasma storm as he pressed up against her, grinding his aching cock against her soft body as he kissed her, showing her how much he needed her. Now that she was finally in his arms and inside the privacy of their home, he needed her so badly it bordered on madness.

He dropped the bag he was carrying to the floor, shrugged out of his jacket, and let it fall, too. He didn't want anything between them anymore. Not the past. Not clothing. Nothing.

"Here?" Dash's voice sounded in his head.

"Right here. Right now."

"And people say I'm *the impetuous one."*

He didn't bother to reply with the internal comm link. "Shut up and get over here. Our angel needs us."

There was so much truth in that one small statement that Mack's words resonated deep inside Lieksa's heart. She did need them. They had been the standard by which she had judged every other male who had tried to win her affection, and not one of them had survived the comparison. There was only room for two men in her heart, and until a few days ago, she had thought they were lost to her forever. She had accepted that her life was going to be one of solitude and penance. Now they were back in her life, maybe there was another future waiting for her. It was more than she dared to hope for.

She couldn't see much of their home past the solid bulk of Mack's body. She caught a glimpse of thick carpeting in dark patterns, creamy walls, and an astounding amount of open space considering they were on a space station. Then the view was blocked again as Mack leaned in for another kiss.

"Welcome to our home, sweetheart," Dash said from somewhere out of sight. "I promise, Mack will let you see some of it eventually," he added with a chuckle.

"I'm not making any *fraxxing* promises," Mack muttered between kisses.

She reached up to stroke his cheek. "We have all night, Mack. I'm not going anywhere."

"Damned right you're not," Dash declared as he moved in beside her.

Once again she was sandwiched between two hard, eager male bodies. She turned toward Dash and Mack claimed the space behind her.

Dash claimed her mouth in a torrid, demanding kiss as Mack swept aside the fall of her hair to lay a fiery path of kisses down the side of her throat. Hands stroked and caressed her all over her body, and she quickly ceased to care who was touching her where. They both moved in closer, letting her feel the hard planes of their bodies and the even harder ridge of their cocks as they ground up against her. Someone cupped her breasts, toying with her aching nipples as Dash's tongue swept into her mouth.

Desires and cravings she didn't know she was capable of swept through her. Every fantasy she'd ever had about the two men holding her came together into a perfect storm of need. She opened herself to the maelstrom, letting it take hold and banishing the last of her doubts and fears.

Strong, calloused hands slid up her thighs, lifting her dress a slow, seductive inch at a time.

"I want to see you, sweetheart. All of you. Are you ready for that?" Dash asked, his hands stopping their upward movement.

She nodded, the small part of her still thinking rationally noting that this was further than they had ever gone. The last time they were together like this, she had stopped them, unwilling to risk being caught.

This time, there was no reason to say no.

Dash's hands began to climb again, while Mack unfastened the back of her dress. The fabric parted, baring her back, and Mack uttered a low groan as his fingers traced the line of her spine.

They undressed her quickly, not bothering to hide their eagerness. The second her panties hit the floor they were shedding their own clothes, and she drank in the sight of them. *Re'veth*, they were gorgeous. Not the biggest cyborgs she'd ever seen, or the bulkiest, but both of them had the hard muscles and strength that was part of every cyborg's design. Dash's physique was leaner than Mack's, and he was slightly shorter. His appearance was an intentional design choice made to let him blend in better with the humans he was supposed to spy on.

Mack finished undressing first and gave her a cocky grin as he caught her staring. Without a word, he took her hand and led her into a cozy living room furnished with several chairs in varying shades of gray and silver, and an old fashioned divan-style couch. He sat down and drew her onto his lap with her back to his chest, her legs resting on top of his. When she reached up to cover herself, he caught her hands in his and drew them back to her sides.

"You don't need to hide from us. Let us show you how beautiful we think you are."

Dash kicked his pants free and joined them, sinking to his knees in front of her. He placed his hands on her thighs, pushing them apart until they dropped to the outsides of Mack's. Mack spread even wider so that she was on display.

"I know we already had one dessert, but I think it's time for another," Dash murmured before moving between her legs and dipping his head to kiss her inner thigh. Each kiss was a little higher than the last, and soon his breath fanned over the swollen lips of her pussy. There was no hiding how aroused she was. Not when she was so slick and eager for him to touch her again.

He parted her lips with his fingers, tracing slow circles around her clit until she gasped and rocked her hips into his hand.

"Do you want him to touch you? Will you let him taste you?" Mack asked, his voice buzzing against the side of her neck.

"Yes. Please, yes. We've waited long enough, haven't we? I want you both so badly." She had never wanted anything as badly as this. The three of them together, fulfilling a promise they'd made a lifetime ago.

"Thank you," Dash whispered, leaned in, and began an oral assault that left her breathless and quivering. He slid a finger into her channel, fucking her slowly as he sucked and lapped at her clit in turns.

Mack released her hands and reached up to play with her breasts, pinching and stroking her tender skin until she felt every one of his touches like a jolt straight to her already throbbing clit.

"Come for us, Lieksa. Scream if you want. No one can hear you. We want to know if you're enjoying yourself.

She laughed. "As if there was any doubt."

"You're even sexier when you laugh. You should do that more often," Dash said before diving back between her thighs to work her clit even more fiercely than before. It was more than she could take, and she came hard a few minutes later, giving voice to her pleasure not because they asked it of her, but because it was too much to hold inside.

Her body was still trembling with the aftershocks of her orgasm when Dash helped her back to her feet. He stole a tender kiss that left the taste of herself on her lips and guided her into a new position, on her hands and knees on the divan with her forearms crossed over the high, curving end. Mack moved in behind her, stroking her back with slow, gentle touches as Dash stepped in front of her, his thick cock fisted in one hand as he gave her a look of pure adoration.

He tangled his fingers in her hair and tipped her head back to look up at him. "Thank you for giving us a second chance, angel,"

"You're welcome," she said, then turned to look back at Mack. "Make this real, Mack. I don't want to live in the past anymore."

Mack nodded and settled in behind her, leaning down to press an open mouthed kiss to her shoulder blade as his cock found her slick entrance. She leaned backward, pushing him deeper, and he groaned as he slid into her body.

Dash kept his hand in her hair as he leaned down to kiss her, his tongue invading her mouth at the same moment Mack surged into her. It was a perfectly timed moment that set fire to her soul.

Her body stretched with delicious slowness, blending pleasure and pain as she accommodated Mack's thick girth. Once he was buried balls-deep he stilled, giving her time to adjust.

"Okay?" he asked.

"Perfect," she wriggled her hips to invite him to move again.

He didn't need much encouragement. He straightened, his hands gripping her hips to hold her steady as he started to move. He kept his thrusts light and shallow at first, but she rocked backward, making it clear she was ready for more, and he complied with a chuckle.

"I'm hanging onto my control by a thread. If you do that again, you're going to find out just how badly I want you."

She turned her head, breaking her kiss with Dash to glance over at Mack. "I won't break. Show me."

"I think we've been challenged, Mack."

"I think so, too." He tightened his hold and moved faster, building up a delicious friction as his cock stroked over nerve endings she didn't know she had.

Dash stood, gave her a wicked grin, and pumped his fist over his cock. When she licked her lips, he did it again, slower this time. The sight sent sparks shimmering down her spine. She lifted her head from her arms and reached for him. "May I?"

He nodded, and when he spoke his words were barely more than a guttural groan. "You never have to ask permission to touch me. Not ever. I want your hands on me as often as possible."

"I'll have to remember that." She gripped his thick shaft and tugged him closer. close enough she could lean forward and run her tongue across the crown of his cock. She moaned as Mack's cock filled her again and again. She couldn't keep her focus on either one. The touch of a hand, the scent of male arousal, the taste of Dash in her mouth, all conspired to make her drunk and dizzy with pleasure.

Dash held still, letting her explore him, but when she pumped his shaft his hips jerked.

His cock pressed against her lips and she opened her mouth. Now she had both of them inside her. Both men groaned, the primal sound turning her on even more.

"Is her mouth as incredible as her pussy?" Mack asked, and his carnal words aroused her even more.

"*Fraxx*, yes," Dash grunted out the words in time to the rocking of his hips as his control slipped another notch.

It was intoxicating to know that she had both men wild with need for her. She used every trick she had ever read or heard about to pleasure them both, flexing around Mack's cock as she stroked and licked the length of Dash's shaft.

They lifted her up to heights of pleasure, pushing her further and higher than she had ever been before.

"Come for us, Lieksa," Mack instructed, driving himself into her with powerful thrusts. He set a merciless pace that made her toes curl and her breath catch in her throat.

Dash stroked her brow with shaking fingers. "I'm so close. If you don't want—" she ignored his warning and reached down to cradle his balls in her hand, pressing a finger to the sensitive spot behind and stroking the skin gently.

His next breath came out as an explosive exhalation, and he came hard, emptying himself into her mouth. Behind her, Mack growled her name, and she felt his cock thicken as he prepared to come as well. He reached between her legs and pressed on her clit, sending her soaring into an orgasm of her own. She was out of control and trembling as both men came, filling her body and claiming her in the most primal of acts.

Mack slumped over her back, his warm weight pressing her down into the cushions as Dash eased himself out of her mouth and dropped to his knees so that his forehead was pressed to hers.

"We should have taken you that night and never let you go," Dash muttered.

"We would never have made it," she whispered back. "We had to let go so we could find each other again. Now, there's no reason we can't be together."

"No reason at all," Mack agreed, his breath warm as it fanned across her skin.

"Together at last," Dash sounded incredibly pleased.

For as long as it lasts, she added to herself, but right now she was too happy to worry about what the future might bring. That was a concern for tomorrow…or maybe the day after that. For a little while at least, she had everything she had ever dreamed of.

CHAPTER EIGHT

It had been a long time since Lieksa felt this happy. In fact, she wasn't sure she had ever felt like this. Everything in her life seemed better since the night of her first and second dates with Mack and Dash. Her fantasies had paled in comparison to the reality of being with them.

They hadn't left the house in twenty-four hours. They spent their time talking and making love by turns. They slept when they were tired, ate when they were hungry, and filled the rest of their time catching up on their lives and learning more about each other. It had been a wonderful, idyllic interlude, and she was sorry it was coming to an end. She wasn't ready to return to reality yet, but they didn't have a choice.

Dash was cleared to return to duty, and both men were needed to lead the taskforce and continue investigating what went wrong during their last raid. There was more to it than either of them were willing to talk about, and while she understood the need for secrecy, it bothered her that there were things she didn't know. Their jobs came with a certain level of risk, but she had a sense that this was something even worse. Tomorrow they would both be back in the line of fire. While many things had changed since the first time they had met, the men she cared for were still warriors who put their lives on the line every day. She was going to have to get used to worrying about them every time they went to work.

The guys were downstairs making a late night snack while she finished dressing. Mack and Dash both had bedrooms bigger than her whole residence, though they had opted to sleep in Mack's room because it had its own small ensuite bathroom. Dash's room was across the hall, and he had offered her a drawer and space in his closet. She didn't have much to put in them, but she put an extra sweater and a pair of socks in the mostly empty drawer before leaving the room. It was a start, and she would add more the next time she was over.

It still amazed her that there would be a next time. That she was actually thinking about a future that involved the three of them. It was too soon to be feeling this hopeful, but she couldn't help herself. She was too happy *not* to hope.

She was coming down the stairs to the main living area when she heard Mack's voice. He was speaking in clipped, sharp tones that made her pause halfway down the stairs to listen.

"Get some officers down to the medical center right away. Len Daniels is still recuperating there, and I don't want him left unguarded. If someone's coming after the members of the taskforce, everyone is going to need to watch their ass. Dash is calling the center right now to let them know they're about to have company. No, the doctor probably isn't going to like it, but she'd like it even less if someone killed one of her patients."

He paused as another voice spoke, but it wasn't clear enough for her to make out what they were saying. "I don't care who you send, sir, so long as you know they're trustworthy. Someone's hunting us, Samson, and they know every *fraxxing* move we make."

There was another short silence before he spoke again. "I'm calling in the entire taskforce. I want them to hear the news from us. We'll be there soon."

Her head spun as she made her way down the rest of the stairs. Someone was hunting the Corp-Sec officers? Who was dead? How? Would they come for Dash and Mack next? Her heart twisted in her chest at the thought of losing them again, and she nearly missed the last step. She stumbled and smacked into a wall of hard muscles.

"Hey, easy there!" Mack said, wrapping her in his arms to steady her.

"Thanks. I'd make a joke about you sweeping me off my feet, but I get the feeling now's not a good time for jokes."

He hugged her hard and buried his face in her hair. "How much did you hear?"

"Enough to guess that someone's dead and you don't think whoever did it is finished hunting down the members of your team. I'm sorry, Mack."

"Thank you. He was our newest member, but he'll be missed all the same. Officer Crews was a good man."

She stiffened. "Officer Steve Crews? You mean Len's partner? He's dead?" She remembered meeting him during one of her brief visits to see Len, and it jarred her to realize she would never see him again.

"How do you know Steve?"

"The medical center isn't that big. I met him once or twice in the hallway, and Len introduced us once when I popped in to say hi."

"You were visiting Len? Why?"

"I met him while I was taking care of Dash, remember? You saw us talking. He asked me to say hi if I was around because he's bored and stuck there for a few more days."

"He's going to lose his mind when he finds out about Crews. *Veth,* I don't want him finding out from the guys I sent to protect him." He raised his voice. "Dash! We need to go. We have to stop by medical on our way in. We need to tell Len what happened and then order him to stay put or he's likely to go on the warpath tonight."

Mack leaned down to kiss her brow, then released her. "You need to stay here, Lieksa. We'll be back when we can."

She shook her head. "I'll go home. You two are going to be busy for the next while, and I don't want to be a distraction."

"No. You're staying put. I don't have time to argue about this with you. You need to stay here where we know you'll be safe."

She bristled, hands settling on her hips as she glowered up at him. "I'm not one of your taskforce, Mack. You can't bark orders at me and expect me to obey. If that's how you think this relationship is going to work, then you're deluded. Go see Len and talk to your task force, I can take care of myself."

He pulled himself to his full height and stared down at her. "You don't understand. Crews wasn't the only one who died tonight. His wife was killed too. You've been out in public with us, which means you're a target, too."

"After one date?"

"We're not willing to take that risk," Dash chimed in as he joined the conversation. "Please, sweetheart. Stay here for now."

Her mother always told her it was important to start as you intended to go on. Their concern was touching, but she wasn't going to let anyone bark orders at her and expect her to obey. Compromise and communication were required if they were going to make this work.

"I have a better idea. What if I came with you? You can leave me at the medical center. You sent guards there, right? I'll be perfectly safe, and I could finish reading over the last of your tests, Dash. It shouldn't be hard to get someone to escort me home from there, either."

Mack scowled, then sighed. "Fine. Grab your things. You can come with us."

"Of course I can. I'm a grown woman who can make her own decisions." Mack was naturally domineering, and that was fine, but he had to accept that as sexy as she found his confidence, that didn't mean she was going to abdicate all say in her own life.

She turned and jogged back up the stairs without giving either of them time to say anything else.

Dash watched her go and then turned to his friend. "Stellar job, Mack. I want to keep her safe as much as you do, but did you really think that was the right approach? Sit. Stay. That's what you tell a pet, not your girlfriend."

"I've never had either of those things," Mack pointed out.

"And it shows. When she gets back down here, do us both a favor and apologize."

"I'm not going to say I'm sorry for trying to protect her. We lost her once, Dash. I don't ever want to go through that again."

Dash's gut twisted at the thought of losing Lieksa. He and Mack had built a good life for themselves, but there had always been something missing. He believed Lieksa was the one who could fill that void. If anything happened to her, he doubted either one of them would ever recover. That didn't give them the right to bark orders, though. "We're never going to stop trying to keep her safe, but that doesn't mean treating her the way we were once treated. She deserves better."

Mack grunted in agreement. "I hate it when you're right. Good thing it doesn't happen all that often."

"I'm almost always right. Clearly, you need your memory banks checked. Maybe Lieksa can run a diagnostic and figure out what's causing your faulty recall."

"There's nothing wrong with my recall. I'm not the one who got himself shot in the head. Speaking of which, do you remember anything new?"

"Nothing useful. Daniels and I, heading up the last ladder to reach the catwalk. Muzzle flash of a weapon being fired at close range. No faces. No recall of how the hell the shooter got the drop on us. Now some son of a starbeast is out there taking out the members of our *fraxxing* task force, and I can't remember anything helpful." He slammed a fist into the wall, giving vent to some of his frustration.

"We'll figure this out and put a stop to it."

"If I could remember what happened, we might have already ended this and Crews would still be alive."

"And if wishes were horses, then beggars would ride," Lieksa said, appearing at the top of the stairs with her bag over her shoulder.

"Why would a beggar want to ride a horse? Eat it, maybe, but ride it?" Mack asked, making both Lieksa and Dash laugh.

"It's a saying my mother used to repeat when I got frustrated about something beyond my control. You can't fix your missing memories just by wishing for them, Dash, but you can get these guys before they hurt anyone else. Focus on that, and maybe the rest will fall into place."

It was sensible advice, but he still wished there was a quick fix, some way to get out ahead of the cartel and take them down for good. "Our angel is sexy, beautiful, and smart as hell. How did we get so lucky, Mack?"

"That's your cue. Say you're sorry," he added on their internal channel.

"I don't know, but I'm glad we did." Mack cleared his throat and turned so that he was looking up at Lieksa. "I'm sorry I tried to pull rank on you. I'm out of practice talking to people who aren't paid to do what I tell them."

She stared at him and burst out giggling. "How many girlfriends have you paid for, exactly?"

"What? No! None. I mean…*fraxx*, that's not what I meant."

Mack was tripping over his words as he tried to explain, and it was the funniest thing Dash had ever seen. He doubled over with laughter.

"You could help me instead of braying with laughter, you know," Mack muttered.

"Oh, hell no. You're on your own." He held out his hand to Lieksa. "You ready to go, sweetheart?"

"I am." Her words were honey-sweet as she took his hand. "You coming, Mack?"

As they left the residence, Dash was struck by two intertwined truths. Lieksa was going to make their lives far more interesting, and he would lay down his own life before he let anything happen to her.

* * * *

By the time the three of them arrived at the medical center, they had briefed Lieksa with enough details to make her understand Mack's behavior, even if it didn't excuse it.

Officer Crews and his wife were shot and killed only a few steps from their residence, and despite the fact they were in a busy corridor, not one witness saw the perpetrator. Whoever the murderer was, they'd managed to get close to the pair, fire off several energy bolts in rapid succession, and vanish into the crowd before anyone could react.

Violence was an ingrained part of life on the Drift, but for the most part, it was bar-brawls and pharma-fueled disruptions by platform workers and asteroid miners. Both groups came to entertainment stations like Astek, to blow off steam. The miners were especially rowdy after months out in the asteroid field with nothing to do but work and dream of their next shore leave. A calculated, cold-blooded hit, like what was done to Crews was rare. And it was made worse because he was Corp-Sec, the only law enforcement for light-years around, who were treated with at least grudging respect by almost everyone on the Drift.

If the details of what happened hadn't been enough, the way both Dash and Mack acted on the trip to Medical had hammered the danger home. They walked with one hand on their weapons, keeping her shielded between them while they scanned their surroundings constantly.

There was a massive Corp-Sec officer guarding the main door. He was far too big to be human, and a quick glance at the barcode imprinted on his wrist confirmed her suspicions. The mountain of muscles poured into a Corp-Sec uniform was a cyborg, and one of the largest she had ever seen. He was also surprisingly scruffy looking for an officer. His dark hair fell to his shoulders, and his beard was in need of a trim.

"Sorry, folks. I'm going to have to ask you for ID before you go inside." The officer held out a handheld scanner.

"Corp-Sec officers Mack Darian and Dash Scudo," Mack stated and placed his hand on the device. His name and image appeared on the screen. Dash went next, but when it was Lieksa's turn the door opened, and an infuriated Alyson arrived.

"Will you stop that? For *veth*'s sake, these are the two idiots who asked you to guard this place, and Lieksa is my friend. I swear to the stars above and below if you don't stop scanning every patient trying to get into the center I'm going to stick that thing somewhere you're going to need a surgeon to have it extracted!" Alyson finished by cursing in two different languages, neither of which Lieksa was familiar with.

"Interesting bedside manner you must have, Dr. Jefferies. If you're vouching for the woman, then of course she can go in. And where did you learn to curse in Jeskyran?"

Mack cleared his throat. "Doc, I know you don't like it, but he's doing his job. The officer who died was Len Daniel's partner. He needs protecting, and so do you."

Alyson frowned. "Don't remind me that this was all your idea, Mack. And you, Dash! You know I treat everyone, including those who would rather not be scanned and identified. Everyone deserves medical treatment, and Officer Overkill and his brothers are making that impossible."

"My name is Blade."

Alyson uttered a strangled choking noise and shook her head. "Of course it is. Lance, Dirk, and

Blade. Whoever named you and your batch brothers didn't get enough hugs as a child."

Blade's lips twitched into a grin beneath his dark beard. "Seeing as how we named ourselves, I'd say your assessment is accurate enough."

Alyson blushed. "Oh. Well then. They're very uh…military names."

Lieksa had to lower her head to hide her grin.

The four of them left Blade outside and headed into the medical center. "Len's in his room. He doesn't know anything concrete, but he suspects something's happened. It's hard to hide three massive Corp-Sec officers, especially when one of them is guarding his door."

"We'll talk to him. The guards aren't just here for your protection. They're to keep Len from doing something stupid, like leaving before you've cleared him to be back on his feet," Dash said.

Alyson sighed. "I know. I don't like it, but I do understand. Len should be ready to go home in two days, but he won't be ready to go back to work for at least another two weeks. He doesn't have a microscopic army of medi-bots to help get him back on his feet."

"We'll make sure he takes the time he needs." Mack turned and smiled at Lieksa. "See you soon, angel."

"Stay inside, please?" Dash added before kissing her.

"I won't take any chances, I promise." Mack spun her into his arms and kissed her, too.

"Thank you," he murmured as he let her go.

"You've got enough on your plates right now. I won't add to it." They needed to stay focused on the threat to their team. She had intended to tell them that she was going to help Alyson find out what had been done to the female cyborgs, but now wasn't the time. She didn't want to lie to them, not even by omission, but they didn't need distractions right now. She would tell them as soon as the immediate threat was dealt with, and lives weren't at stake any longer.

"When you're ready to go home, call one of us, and we'll arrange an escort," Mack told her.

"We'll try and come ourselves," Dash added.

They went straight to Len's room, passing another massive Corp-Sec officer who appeared to be a duplicate of Officer Blade. The moment the door closed Alyson turned to Lieksa, eyebrows raised and a broad smile on her face.

"You make a cute trio, and I've never seen Mack act like that. You make him happy. It's nice to see."

Lieksa lowered her voice. "Thanks. Early days yet, but our first date went so well it kind of turned into a second. And a sleepover."

"Wow. Those two didn't waste any time, did they? Someday soon you and I are going for a drink, and you can tell me all about it."

"You're on, but only if you tell me why Blade and his batch brothers have you all flustered."

Alyson groaned. "They're not just brothers, they're triplets. Three identical, hulking, annoying, incredibly bossy men who waltzed into my med-center and tried to take over," she huffed in indignation and jerked her head toward the brother still standing guard outside Len's door. "That's Dirk. He's the bossiest of the three."

"That's because I'm the oldest," Dirk called out. Unlike Blade, he was clean-shaven, which made it easy to spot the way he was smirking as he interjected.

Alyson cursed softly and rounded on the big cyborg. "It's not nice to eavesdrop on a private conversation. And don't you try that old excuse about how it's not your fault that cyborgs have superior hearing."

Dirk actually looked surprised. "But we do."

"True or not, it's bad manners," the doctor informed him, then turned to Lieksa. "Let's go to my office."

"I was going to suggest that. I've got a few more questions for you about that little project we were discussing."

Alyson nodded and led the way to her office. Once they were behind closed doors, she burst out laughing. "I get the feeling none of them have ever been told to mind their manners before."

"He did look surprised when you called him on it. I swear they're all too bossy for their own good. Mack actually tried to order me to stay at his place because it might not be safe for me."

Alyson shook her head. "If you're serious about taking on the two of them, you're going to need some expert advice. Cynder's known your guys for a few years, and Zura's married to another pair of cyborgs. You've already met them, right? They both visited Dash a couple of times."

"Cynder's the gorgeous, long-legged cyborg, right? And Zura was the quiet little half-Pheran. I remember them."

Alyson chortled. "Zura's only quiet until you get to know her. She manages her bossy cyborg husbands very nicely, which is why I think we need a girls' night, soon." Her gaze drifted to the door. "Just in case I lose my mind and do something foolish, it might be smart to get a few pointers."

"I'd really like that. I haven't had a girls' night out since I got here. In fact, I really haven't been out much at all."

"Then leave it to me to arrange things," Alyson said, gesturing around her office. "I need to get out of here and have some fun. Or so Cynder informed me the last time she was here."

"She's right. I've spent the last few days here, and I swear you never go home. You do need to rest sometimes, Doc."

"I do go home. As it happens, home is one level up. The doctor who set this place up arranged the living situation for himself, and when I bought him out, I got his residence, too."

"Nice setup. It keeps you close at hand in case your patients need you. The hospital ship I worked on had a similar setup. Living quarters were always close to our assigned wards."

Alyson leaned forward in her chair. "I've been meaning to ask you about that. You tell everyone you're a lab tech, but I saw you work on Dash, and I have to say, I've seen doctors with less skill than you. You're a lot more than just a tech, aren't you?"

She shrugged. "Lab-tech is the general term for what I was. The reality is more complicated. I repaired, designed, and installed cybernetic implants for soldiers in a hospital ship that treated our wounded. I guess I'm somewhere between a robotics engineer and a surgeon. It's a very specialized profession, and I haven't done it since the night I learned my subjects were human beings. These days, I really am a simple tech. I keep Astek's fleet of in-house bots and automated systems running. Nothing life or death about it, and I know my patients can't experience pain or fear. It's better that way."

With that, Lieksa shifted the topic. "I'm going back to work tomorrow, so I should be able to start looking for answers about what was done to the female cyborgs. I was hoping we could go through everything again."

Alyson nodded and pulled out a data tablet, setting it on the desk between them before activating its holographic display. "I'm guessing it would be best if I don't know exactly how you're getting this information, right?"

Lieksa shrugged. "I'm not doing anything too nefarious. My security clearance is relatively good. I'm going to start with the easy places and hope I get lucky." The odds that the information she needed was somewhere easy to find were worse than a snowball's chance in a supernova, but she had to start somewhere. If that failed, her workshop was full of spare parts and miscellaneous tech, including a black-market data-mining widget. All it had to do was get close to the source. She had removed it from a corporate executive's personal aid droid months ago but hadn't gotten around to destroying it, yet.

There wasn't much difference between the widget and the cybernetic implants Dash used to scan and steal digital data. She could reactivate and install it on a maintenance bot currently waiting to be repaired. The bot had access to every level of Astek's offices. If she could tell it what to scan for, it was her best bet at finding the answers they were looking for.

As the doctor started speaking, Lieksa focused on every word, committing them to memory. This was a chance to help the cyborgs, and take another step toward redeeming herself in the process.

CHAPTER NINE

Dash stared at Mack in disbelief. "What do you mean, you're not coming? We've only seen Lieksa once this week. If you try and tell me you don't miss her, I'll kick your ass and call you a liar."

Mack glanced up from his monitor and sighed. "Of course I miss her. And I didn't say I wasn't coming, I said I would be along in a while. I need to finalize this paperwork first, though."

"Priorities, Mack. We need to work on your *fraxxing* priorities." It was an argument that had come up more than once during the last few days. Dash wanted to spend time with Lieksa, but something was holding Mack back. He didn't understand it. This was only going to work if the three of them were a true trio. He'd seen how it could be when everything came together, and he wanted that. He wanted what their friends Kit and Luke had with Zura, and what Cynder had found with her new husbands.

"My priority is to catch the bastards trying to kill us. Once that's happened, I can think about Lieksa and the future. If something happened to her, I'd never forgive myself."

"If you keep pulling away from her, there might not be a future for us. Don't let this destroy our chance with her, Mack. If you do that, I may never forgive *you*."

"Twenty minutes. Give me twenty minutes, and I'll be there, I promise."

"You better be."

Dash left their shared office, stopping for a few minutes to chat with the taskforce members working in their squad room. They were all in a dark mood, full of frustration and struggling to deal with the loss of their teammate, so he ordered all of them to take a long lunch and try to relax a little. They left the building together, and on the walk out he was struck by the change in the whole department. The atmosphere these days was subdued. The friendly banter and smiles were gone, replaced by wary expressions and hushed conversations. The service for Crews and his wife the previous evening had been a quiet, private affair organized quickly and done with minimal fanfare. Crews deserved better, but anything more public would have put everyone attending at risk.

There hadn't been another attack in the days after Crews' murder and things were calming down, though the constant need to be on guard weighed on everyone. Corp-Sec offices across the

Drift were working together, tracking down any lead and working every angle, but so far the Drojo Cartel was as elusive as smoke in a ventilator shaft. For Dash, the threat of another attack and his own recent brush with death made it clear to him where he wanted to be, and with whom. Mack was dealing with it in a different way, working long hours and chasing data, looking for the answers, trying to find a way to regain control of the situation. It didn't usually bother Dash to see Mack get like this, but this time there was too much on the line.

Once he was out of headquarters, his mood lightened, and he pushed the gloomy thoughts to the back of his mind. He crossed the crowded causeway and headed for one of their preferred food vendors to pick up the order he had made this morning. The plan had been to surprise Lieksa with an impromptu picnic at her workshop. Mack's decision to stay a little longer wouldn't throw things too far off track. In fact, Dash's head was already full of ideas on how he and Lieksa could spend the time waiting for Mack, and not one of them included eating lunch. He was definitely in a 'life is short, eat dessert first,' kind of mood.

* * * *

Lieksa was elbows-deep in a maintenance bot's innards when the door to her workshop opened. "If you're bringing me yet another damaged unit,

Zale, I swear I'm going to start jettisoning them out the nearest airlock and claiming they were lost in transit."

"That's an interesting way to greet visitors. As it happens, I come bearing gifts of food for the sexiest tech on the station."

Her head snapped up, and she dropped everything to bound across the room, only to stop a foot away when she remembered she was covered in grime. Dash looked hot as hell in his uniform, and she didn't want to mess it up. "Hi! Welcome to the land of broken toys."

"Hi, sweetheart. I thought it was about time we saw where you worked." He closed the distance between them in a single stride and wrapped an arm around her, pulling her in close before kissing her hello.

The second he touched her she melted into his arms and kissed him back, rising up on her toes to twine her arms around his neck. It felt like it had been ages since she had been in Dash's arms, even though it had only been two days.

"Now that's the kind of welcome a man could get used to," Dash murmured the next time he came up for air.

"Your uniform is going to wind up with permanent stains that way."

His lips curved up into a wicked little smile. "There's an easy fix for that. No stains if you take off the work clothes before saying hello."

"I'm not getting naked in my workshop." She gestured to the cluttered metal surfaces and shelves full of out of service bots and spare parts. "Too many pointy, sharp things in here, for one thing."

"I solemnly swear that whenever and wherever you are naked, Mack and I will protect you from all things cold, sharp, or pointed."

A pang of disappointment dampened her good mood. "I'd be more likely to believe that if Mack was here to speak for himself. He's still at headquarters, isn't he?" Mack seemed to spend every waking moment working. While she understood the need driving him, it was starting to feel like he was using the work as a way to keep some distance between them.

"He'll be here soon. We planned this little surprise together. He had one more report to finish reading, that's all." Dash stroked his fingers down her cheek and bowed his head to nuzzle her cheek. "I've missed you."

"I missed you, too," she confessed in a low murmur before forcing herself to adopt a light, breezy tone. "I'm glad you're here, and with food, too. No one's ever brought me lunch before. You're going to spoil me. If you let me go, I'll clear off a place for us to eat."

"I'm not ready to let go of you, yet. The way I see it, we've got a couple of choices. One, you can give me the grand tour of your workplace while we wait for Mack to get here. Two, we eat now, and he can forage for leftovers when he arrives.

Three, we do something to light a fire under Mack's ass. Personally, I'm a fan of option number three."

She lifted her arm and gestured around them. "We can take the tour without moving. Behold my workspace in its entirety. So, I think I'd like to hear more about option three. What was your plan?"

He smirked and waggled his brows. "You and I get naked and enjoy some mind-blowing sex, which I will relay to Mack in real time. I guarantee that will launch him out of his office and on a direct course for this place at light-speed. You game?"

Suddenly she didn't care about propriety. "Now is when I remind you that you vowed to protect me from all things sharp and pointy while naked."

He cradled her in his arms, and when he spoke his words held a note of truth that resonated deep in her heart. "I will always protect you, Lieksa. You're the most precious thing in my life."

Words failed her, and the lump in her throat would have made it impossible for her to speak anyway, so she answered the only way she could; she held him tight and kissed him. It was a wild, passionate kiss driven by the tumult of emotions churning inside her. There were tears on her cheeks as he lifted her into his arms, her name a low groan on his lips as he took everything she offered him, devouring her, body and soul.

They were locked together, mouths fused, limbs wrapped around each other—even their breaths were shared. At that moment, she knew she was falling for them, and that knowledge sent her heart soaring into an orbit so high she would never survive re-entry.

Somehow Dash managed to keep hold of her while finding an empty shelf to stash the meal she had forgotten he was holding. Once both of his hands were free, he carried her back to her workbench and cleared off a corner, knocking everything to the ground with a clatter.

"I hope none of that was important," he said as he set her down on the newly cleared space.

"If it is, I'll just repair it again," she said.

"I love a woman who is good with her hands."

"That's because these hands have saved your sexy ass, twice," she replied, waving her fingers in the air. It was a lame response, but her brain misfired the moment Dash uttered the word love. It didn't matter he hadn't meant it as a declaration. After her recent emotional revelation, simply hearing the word was enough to cause a short circuit.

"You think my ass is sexy, huh?" he asked as he tore away the stained, lightweight coverall she wore to protect her clothes.

"I think you're sexy from head to toe. I have since the first time I examined you. You were flirting with me, which I found totally distracting. I'd never worked on an infiltration unit—cyborg before you." She corrected herself quickly.

"Unit. Cyborg. Lover. I don't care what you call me because I know you're talking about me as a man, not a machine."

He was easing her out of her regular clothes now, keeping her distracted with kisses and caresses as he worked.

"Not just a man. My man," she clarified, reaching out to rest her hand over his heart so she could feel it beat against her palm.

"Yeah, I'm all yours. And you're all mine. From your cute toes to this glorious mane of red hair. Mine." He wrapped a strand of her hair around his finger and tugged gently. "I dreamed about doing this so many times."

"Pulling my hair?" she asked, laughing now.

"Playing with your hair. Laughing with you. Stripping you naked so I could make love to you. The day we learned the *Salan* had been destroyed with all hands on board, a piece of my heart went dark."

"The ship was destroyed the day after my resignation and your transfer. I just wish…" she trailed off and kissed him again. Regret wouldn't change what happened. The time they had lost was gone, and there was no getting it back.

"You're here. I'm here. That's all that matters." He lifted her off her perch and set her back on her feet so that he could finish removing her clothes. Once she was naked, he stripped off the top half of his uniform and laid it on the workbench.

"To make sure you don't get cold," he said before boosting her back into the same spot.

"And to be sure we're not interrupted, I'll get the door," she said and then raised her voice to address the workshop's AI. "Computer, please secure the workshop door."

"Yes, Technician Kiv. The door is now secured."

"Technician Kiv, did you just lock Mack out of this workshop?" Dash asked with a wicked chuckle as he shed the rest of his clothes.

"Yes, I did. If he wants in, he's going to have to knock and ask nicely." She should have locked it earlier, but she had been distracted by Dash's kisses.

"Then let's give him a reason to get here so I can see his face when you finally let him in."

"Speaking of seeing, I think it's time you gave him a sample of what he's missing out on."

Dash took a step back and raked his heated gaze over her, clearly enjoying himself. "I'm opening the link now."

While he was communicating with their missing partner, she indulged in a long, leisurely perusal of the man standing in front of her. A body like his should be illegal. He could have been forged from steel or sculpted in marble by a master artist, and in a way, he had been. He was a masterpiece of genetic manipulation and biotechnology, and sexy as sin, too.

"Tell him to hurry," she murmured, reaching for Dash.

"He heard you," Dash said, then moved in close, his eyes never leaving hers as he dropped a scorching kiss to her lips.

He parted her legs with one hand, positioning himself between her thighs. She was on display for him, wet and aching with the need to be touched. "Need you," she whispered, aware that Mack would hear every word she said.

"Tell me what you need from me, sweetheart. I want to hear it."

"Touch me."

"Touch you where, exactly? Here?" He palmed her breasts, and her nipples tightened into diamond-hard peaks.

"Not there. Lower."

"You want me to fuck your pussy with my fingers? Make you come all over my hand?"

His words inflamed her, and so did the fact that Mack was seeing and hearing everything they did. She wasn't one for public displays, but this was a private show. She nodded, but Dash shook his head.

"If you want me to touch you, sweetheart. You need to say the words."

"I want you to make me come all over your hand."

Dash groaned, and his cock went rock hard in an instant. "Hands on the counter behind you.

That's right, lean back and show me that pretty pussy."

She felt a dark thrill chase down her spine as she did what he instructed. Both of them loved it when she let them take command during sex. It turned them on, and knowing she could do that for them was a turn-on for her. She settled back on her hands, arched her back and spread her legs wider, giving him exactly what he wanted.

"So sexy." He left one hand on her breast while the other drifted slowly down her body, bypassing her pussy to trace a swirling pattern across the damp skin of her inner thigh. "You're so wet for me right now."

"Just for you."

Dash chuckled. "Oh sweetheart, he didn't like that at all. Mack says I'm a bastard and you are going to pay for that when he gets here. He's on his way."

"Then you better hurry up and enjoy these few minutes you have me all to yourself."

He growled low in his throat and cupped her sex in his hand. "All mine."

"I am."

Her words seemed to set Dash free. His fingers plunged into her slick folds, seeking out her clit and capturing it between thumb and forefinger. There was nothing gentle or teasing about his touch. He was on a mission to bring her to orgasm. He worked the delicate cluster of nerves with the precision of a surgeon, pushing her up the scales of pleasure so quickly it was all she could do to remember to breathe.

He fucked her with deft fingers, first one, then two, curving them the perfect amount to make her gasp every time he brushed over the sensitive spot inside her. He added a third, filling her to the point of pain without quite crossing the line. She leaned back even further so she could lift her hips from the table, meeting his thrusts and taking him deeper.

He pressed his thumb hard against her clit, and she cried out as the pleasure became more than she could take. A few more strokes and she was trembling on the verge of orgasm, her body primed and ready. He took her over with a twist of his fingers, sending her flying.

She was still caught in the aftershocks when he lifted her legs and wrapped them around his waist. "I need you."

She managed a shaky nod, and he buried himself inside her in one long, slow push that nearly triggered another orgasm. She sat up, latching onto him as he took her into his arms. He moved with punishing power, his strokes wild and uneven as he gave up all pretense of control.

Lifting her higher, he buried his face into the crook of her neck and groaned her name, the sound muffled against her skin.

Primal instincts rose inside her, and she scored his back with her nails, urging him on. She rode his body hard, taking everything he gave her and giving him all of herself in return. His cock jerked deep inside her, and his body stiffened as his release came on with the force of a booster rocket.

"You undo me, angel," he told her, his voice a ragged whisper as he cradled her in his arms.

"There's no one in all the worlds who make me feel the way you and Mack do."

He held her tight, whispering a litany of soft words that filled her heart with shimmering bubbles of pure joy.

* * * *

Mack was out of his chair less than ten seconds after Dash opened the link and flooded his mind with sensations: sights, sounds, and flashes of scent and touch. He cursed Dash in six different languages as he realized what his partner was doing.

Normally he would make sure he was seated and still during an open-link session like this, but this time he didn't have that choice. He could either cut the link and deprive himself of the experience, or try to make it to Lieksa's workshop while his mind was bombarded with an erotic display that had his cock hard enough to drill through the station's hull-plating.

He was going to *fraxxing* kill Dash for this— right after he made Lieksa scream his name as she came all over his dick.

Thankfully the squad room was empty, which meant there were no witnesses to his hurried departure or the fact he bumped into two desks and a chair on his way out. He had no depth perception when he was linked to Dash in real time; even with the cybernetic enhancements, there were limits to what his brain and body could process. It had damned near gotten him killed more than once.

He managed to get out of headquarters without any serious problems. Navigating the bustling crowd on the causeway was more of a challenge, but he would have run naked through a plasma storm if it was the only way to get to Lieksa.

Forced to keep his pace to a steady walk, he experienced every second of his partner's seduction of their girlfriend. Frustrated with himself for missing out, he swore that next time he wouldn't let anything distract him from the one source of light and happiness in his life right now. That determination only strengthened when he caught Lieksa's whispered words about the way he and Dash made her feel. He broke into a jog, but only made it a few steps before the deck beneath his feet lurched and he stumbled.

At first, he blamed his lack of depth perception for his misstep. Once he regained his balance and looked around, he knew that wasn't the problem. The wail of alarms and sirens shattered the air, and everywhere he looked people appeared dazed and off-balance.

"What was that?" Dash asked via their internal comm channel even as he severed the shared link between them, freeing up Mack's senses.

"No idea. You and Lieksa okay?"

"We're fine. You?"

"I'm good. Stay with her. I'm going to find out what the fraxx *happened."*

There was a pause before Dash replied. *"Our angel just threw my ass out of her workshop and told me to make sure both of us come back in one piece. She's barely giving me time to get dressed first."*

"Meet me back at HQ."

He didn't like the idea of Lieksa being left alone, but she was right. She was currently in the lower levels of the station's largest complex. She was safer than anywhere else they could take her, except maybe their own offices. He started to scan the area, looking for the source of the sirens, and his heart twisted when he realized they were coming from the one place he would have never expected. Corp-Sec's headquarters.

Personnel started pouring out the main doors, accompanied by an acrid cloud of dark smoke. Some of the officers were limping, others were bleeding, and they all looked shaken by whatever they'd experienced. *Re'veth.* Someone had dared to attack the Corp-Sec headquarters.

This wasn't a hunt anymore. It was a war.

CHAPTER TEN

Lieksa was curled up in one of the chairs in Mack and Dash's living room while the two of them circled around her like Terran sharks. "It doesn't matter how many times you ask me, the answer isn't going to change. I'm not leaving the station. Not for a week, or a day, or even a couple of hours. I'm not the one with a bullseye on my back. Yesterday someone blew up your *fraxxing* squad room. If anyone needs to get away from here for a while, it's the two of you."

"We can't go. We have to stay here and solve this," Dash told her as he passed in front of her again.

She folded her arms over her chest and shook her head. "No, you don't have to stay. You want to, and that's not the same thing. *Veth*, you don't even have an office to work out of right now, because yours was wrecked by the explosion. Here's my deal. If you go, I'll go with you. That's the only way you're getting me off this station."

"Astek isn't safe right now. You wouldn't be the only one going away for a while. A lot of the other task force members have arranged for their families to leave. We talked to a pilot this morning. Her name is Phylomenia and she's an old family friend of Zura's. In fact, she's one of her pilots. Phyl's got some bots and systems that are in disrepair and she would be happy to have you onboard her ship. It's all arranged. You'll go with her on her next delivery run, do some repairs, and by the time you get back, this should all be over."

"You made these arrangements without even talking to me? What about my job? This isn't your decision to make, it's mine, and I'm not going anywhere." She couldn't believe they thought she would meekly get on a ship and fly away.

"Damn it, Lieksa, why can't you understand what's at stake?" Mack snapped at her.

He'd run his hand through his hair so many times that it was standing on end. She understood his concerns, but that didn't make it okay for them to take over her life.

"Don't treat me like an idiot, Mack. I know it's dangerous to stay here. Someone planted a micro-explosive in a get well gift for Len and almost took out your entire team yesterday! If Dash hadn't sent them out for lunch, they'd be dead right now. If we hadn't tempted you away from your desk, you'd be dead. I nearly lost you!" Her voice cracked as she finally uttered the words that had been haunting her since she had learned what happened.

"I'm not treating you like an idiot! We're trying to get you out of the line of fire. This is escalating fast. It's only a matter of time before there's another attack, and I can't do my job if I'm distracted by worries that my girlfriend is a target."

"Even if I were on someone's hit list, it's not like I'm an easy target. My workplace is locked down tight these days, and you've made sure either you, Dash or one of your officers is watching over me the rest of the time. Isn't that enough? I want to stay. My life, my job, and my boyfriends are here. The two of you aren't even guarded, which is insane, considering you're the heads of the task force and therefore are wearing the biggest bullseyes."

"We need to be visible. If someone is going to be attacked, we want it to be us," Mack said.

"What?! You're bait? That's insane. And it's a double standard. You can't order me off the station for my safety when you're taking huge risks yourself."

"All the more reason we need you safely away from here. We can take care of ourselves," Dash said.

"And I can't?" She pointed at Dash. "I'm not the one who was shot recently."

"No, you're the one who saved my life. The only one who could have, which means if they try again, they're not going to want you around to put us back together again." Dash tapped his temple in frustration. "If I could *fraxxing* remember the attack, we'd be that much closer to figuring out what happened, and how they knew we were coming."

"What do you mean, they knew you were coming? I think it's time you told me what really happened that day." She was too angry to agree with him, even if he did have a point.

"It was an ambush. Lucky for us, it wasn't a very good one. The only ones hurt were Dash and Len. Whatever they intended for us, it didn't go as planned."

Icy tendrils of fear wrapped around her chest and squeezed until it felt like she couldn't breathe as they confirmed her suspicions. "Someone told them you were coming. Someone you trusted."

Mack nodded. "We think so."

"And you didn't tell me any of this? I thought we agreed not to keep secrets from each other anymore?"

"That's not a card you want to play," Dash warned her with a quick shake of his head.

"And what's that supposed to mean?"

"It means we know what you're doing for the doc. When, exactly, were you going to tell us you're trying to dig up information about the cyborg program?" Mack asked, his voice as cold as the black void outside the hull.

"How do you know about that?"

"I overheard you talking to Alyson about it," Dash admitted. "You're taking a huge risk. I understand why you're doing it. You've been helping cyborgs for years. It's part of who you are, and you're amazing. That doesn't make what you're doing smart. Do you know what would happen if you got caught? You should have told us. We could have helped you. Data retrieval is our specialty, remember?"

"How could I forget when you just admitted to spying on me?" She spun around to glower at Mack. "Did you know he did that?"

He didn't answer, but the flash of guilt in his eyes told her everything she needed to know.

"You did. I bet he even linked with you so you could both listen in, just like you did when you were sneaking around during the wars. You haven't changed at all, either of you! You're still barking orders and listening in on private conversations. You're supposed to be the good guys, but right now I don't see it."

"Angel—" Mack took a step toward her, but she backed away from him, not interested in anything he had to say.

"Don't call me that. In fact, don't talk to me at all. You've both said more than enough already. You spied on me, you made arrangements to take me off the station without even asking, and neither of you will listen to me. This is my life, and I'm the only one who gets to make the decisions. If you want this to work, then you're going to have to accept that." She turned and walked away.

She only got a few steps before both of them were in pursuit. "Where are you going?" Mack asked.

"I don't know," she snapped.

"You need an escort. Please, let one of us—"

"No."

"It's not safe," Mack reminded her, his tone softer now.

"I'll take my chances."

"Please, don't go." Mack stepped in front of her, blocking her path to the door.

"The last time the two of you hurt me, you said please, and I stayed. That only works once. Get out of my way, Mack. I don't want to talk about this anymore. Not tonight."

"Tomorrow, then. Promise me you'll talk to us tomorrow?" he said.

She saw a flicker of doubt in his eyes as he stood in front of her, arms at his sides, his face showing the strain of the past twenty-four hours. That tiny hint of doubt was the first time she'd ever seen him uncertain about anything, but it wasn't enough to cool her anger.

"Tomorrow," she walked around Mack, half expecting him to reach out and stop her, but he didn't. He didn't move at all.

Dash called out from somewhere behind her. "I know it's not enough, but I'm sorry. I was afraid I'd screwed things up with us, so I listened in when I shouldn't have. It's what I'm programmed to do."

"You can't use your programming as an excuse. You managed to overcome all your other conditioning. You could have overcome this one. You just didn't want to."

"I haven't done it since, and you have my word, I won't do it again."

She didn't answer. She didn't know what to say. All she knew was that she needed to be away from them for a little while.

She left their place and started walking, aimlessly wandering the station for a while as she slowly calmed down.

Eventually, she wound up outside the medical center. Alyson was one of Lieksa's few friends on the station and right now, a friend was exactly what she needed.

* * * *

Mack stood and watched as the center of his universe walked out the door. If he moved or spoke, he would only wind up saying or doing something to make things worse. The second the door slid shut, he turned to look at Dash. "Tell me you have a plan to fix this."

Dash was quiet for a while, but when he spoke, his question took Mack by surprise.

"If you love her, what's with all the distance? I noticed what you were doing, and I'm not the one you claim to be falling for. Holding back and then barking orders at her is no way to treat the woman you care about. I might have eavesdropped on a private conversation, but you're the one who really hurt her. You should have been with us yesterday. Why weren't you?"

There was no missing the accusation buried in his words. The barbs stung, and Mack spoke without thinking, revealing something to himself in the process. "I wasn't there because I was trying to figure out who our mole is before they come after Lieksa, or you for that matter. You two are the most important people in my life. You nearly got killed last week, and I wasn't there to stop it. I let you down, and I'll be damned if I'm going to fail Lieksa the same way."

"You didn't fail anyone. Is that's what this has all been about? You're feeling guilty because I got hurt? Mack, I hate to break it to you, but you're not responsible for everything that goes wrong on this station. We lead the task force together. We've both been betrayed by someone we trusted, and we're both head over heels for a woman who currently would like to see us sucking vacuum on the wrong side of an airlock." Dash slapped a hand on his shoulder and chuckled. "We got here together, my friend, and we'll fix it the same way. Stop thinking you're in this fight alone. Every time you beat yourself up over what happened, or what might happen, you're hurting our angel, too."

Mack felt like his whole existence was spinning out of control. He was happiest when there was an order to things, a linear progression of events.

From the moment they walked into that ambush, nothing was going according to plan. He didn't have a plan anymore. He was running from crisis to crisis. It had to stop before he ruined the only good things in his life. It was time for a change in tactics.

"I know that expression. You've got an idea. Please, tell me you have a brilliant idea," Dash said.

It wasn't an idea, exactly, but it was a start of one. "I was thinking that since my way isn't working, maybe it's time we started doing things your way instead."

Dash shot him a look of pure incredulity. "I don't have a way, remember? I make things up as I go and try not to get shot at. That's your brilliant idea?"

"The mole is expecting us to do things by the book, so our best chance of catching them is to do something unexpected." He went to the front door and scanned the corridor until he spotted Lieksa. She was walking slowly, her head bowed, and her shoulders slumped. "As for fixing things with Lieksa, I don't think we need a plan for that. We need to give her a little time, and tell her how we feel about her."

Dash exhaled in a whoosh. "And if that doesn't work?"

"Then we keep showing her it's true until she believes us." She had to believe them because the idea of living his life without her in it made his heart ache. He'd find a way to make this right. He had to.

"I think I liked it better when you came up with a real plan and left the adlibbing to me."

"Me, too, but since none of our usual ploys are working, I think it's time to play a wild card." It was the only card they had left. After years of reviewing all the data and analyzing every variable, Mack was left relying on his gut—and his heart.

CHAPTER ELEVEN

Alyson's prescription for heartache turned out to be something quite different from what Lieksa expected. Instead of girl talk and junk food, the good doctor took one look at her and announced they were going out for a drink.

"I've got work in the morning," Lieksa protested as she followed Alyson through the med-center.

"So do I. Next excuse? I'm giving you three, so choose wisely."

"I'm not dressed for a night out."

Alyson snorted. "Trust me, where we're going, they won't care. Come on upstairs. You can tidy up while I get changed. As relaxed as the dress code is at Nova, pajamas might be pushing it a bit."

"The Nova? Isn't that Cynder's club?"

"It is. Well, it's one-third hers. She runs the place with her batch brothers, Kit and Luke, who are married to Zura. I don't think you've met them, yet. They're dying to meet you, though." Alyson grinned and pressed a panel on the back wall. It lit up a soft red, and a moment later the wall in front of them slid back, revealing a small elevator.

"Why would anyone want to meet me? I'm nobody."

Alyson raised a blonde brow and gestured for Lieksa to get into the elevator. "You're hardly a nobody. You saved Dash's life for one thing. Not to mention you're dating Mack and Dash."

"I walked out on them tonight after a fight," she admitted.

"So? You're still dating them. One fight doesn't usually mean a relationship is over. If it did, my parents would have left each other decades ago. Besides, I've seen the way they look at you, and that's not the kind of fire that you can snuff out easily. You've still got one excuse left. Care to use it, or are you going to give in gracefully?"

Laughing, Lieksa raised her hands in surrender. "I'm going to give in to the inevitable. Apparently, I'm going out for a drink. Now I know how your patients feel. I bet everyone listens to you."

"Most of the time, they do. With three notable and exceptionally irritating exceptions."

"You mean the overkill triplets?"

"Uh huh. Did you know they insisted on sticking around even after I sent Len home? I had to call Mack to get them out of here."

"He mentioned they were joining the taskforce. In fact, that's sort of how the whole fight started."

"Hold that thought until we get to Nova. That way you only have to tell the story once." Alyson stepped off the elevator and opened her arms. "Welcome to my refuge from reality."

Alyson's residence was large by station standards, with old fashioned furniture and décor that was better suited to a rustic cabin back on Earth. The furniture was heavy and looked like it was made of rough-hewn logs, though a quick brush of her fingers over the surface dispelled the illusion. It was the same molded material as most furnishings on the station. A patchwork quilt lay over the back of the sofa, and there were homey touches everywhere, pictures and bric-a-brac that softened the space and made it feel welcoming. One of the walls was a full-sized vid screen that displayed as a cabin wall, complete with a picture window overlooking a snow-covered valley bathed in moonlight.

"That's incredible. Is it a real place or only a digital fantasy?" Lieksa asked, crossing the room to stare out the 'window' to the scene outside.

"The base image is from my grandparent's place on Cassien Alpha. My parents moved to the city before I was born, but my mom's parents lived in one of the rural outposts. I loved visiting them for holidays, especially during the winter. We'd celebrate the Festival of Light with them every year. The cabin would be full of candles and lights, and we'd stay up all night telling stories, eating and drinking until we could burst. Then we'd watch the sun come up after the longest night of the year. Alyson sighed. "I miss having seasons, or weather of any kind, especially snow."

"I've never seen snow, except in vids and photos. I grew up in Earth's southern hemisphere, where it's too warm for any real winter weather. Not that I saw the outside world much. We lived in New Rio, a hive city. Do you know what those are?"

"I've never been to Earth, but I've heard the stories. Hive cities are so crowded they make this place look like a resort. Aren't they self-contained, too?"

"Pretty much. It made it easy to adjust to life in space. I've spent most of my life in enclosed spaces. Artificial sunlight and recycled air are nothing new. The corporations recruit heavily from the hive cities for that reason. It's an entire population already conditioned to live in space; willing and eager to sign on for any job that pays in real scrip instead of vouchers. They can take their pick."

"Is that how you ended up working on cyborgs?"

"I applied for aptitude testing the day I turned eighteen. Took all the tests, went to an insane number of interviews, and a month later I was recruited by Nobar Tech. I had only recently paid off my training fees and was starting to earn real money when I met Mack and Dash. Once I knew the truth about the cyborgs, I quit."

"And now you're here. We're both a long way from home." Alyson smiled and pointed to a door. "You can freshen up in there. I'm going to let Cyn and Zura know we're coming. Once we've got a drink in your hand, I want to hear all about what happened tonight. I'll even buy the first round."

Lieksa walked in the direction Alyson had pointed, happy for the opportunity to wash away any remaining signs of her earlier tears. She had hurt more in the last two weeks than in the last two years, and it was all because of her two cyborg lovers. The thing was, they made her happier than she had ever been, too. If this was a normal relationship, then maybe they wouldn't be having these problems, but nothing about their relationship had ever been normal. It had been a rocket-boosted roller coaster ride from the moment of their first kiss.

* * * *

Dash didn't take an easy breath until Lieksa was safe indoors. They had followed her, of course. They were careful to keep enough distance between them that they wouldn't be spotted. She may not want to speak to them, but there was no way in hell they'd let her wander the station alone. The medical center wasn't where he expected her to go, but after wandering the station for almost an hour, that's where she finally stopped.

"Do you think she'll stay there long?" Mack asked.

"I don't know. If we contact Alyson, she's going to know we followed Lieksa here. I don't see that going over well, do you?"

Mack snorted. "Not likely, which means either we sit out here like a pair of creepy stalkers, or we admit that we can't protect her every second of the day and night and leave. I don't like either option."

"Neither do I."

They stood in silence for a minute, then Mack elbowed him and pointed. "Is that who I think it is?"

Dash chuckled as he spotted Blade leaning against an alley wall. The big cyborg was almost completely cloaked in shadow. To a normal human he'd be invisible, but cybernetic implants granted most of their kind the ability to see in almost total darkness. "Their guard duty ended when Len was released. What do you think he's doing?"

"The same thing we are. Apparently, we're not the only overprotective ones on the station." Mack folded his arms over his chest and lapsed into a thoughtful silence.

"You think he'd look out for Lieksa tonight, too? That way we could give her the space she needs and still know she's safe."

"That's exactly what I'm thinking. Shall we ask him?"

They joined Blade in the alley, and Dash listened in as Mack briefly explained the situation.

Blade agreed immediately. He also revealed the reason he and his brothers were watching over Alyson. While they were guarding Len, a couple of corporate bureaucrats had come to see the doctor. After they had left, Alyson had looked shaken and extremely pissed. The brothers decided to keep an eye on her, just in case.

They thanked Blade and left. Once they were alone again, Mack grunted in frustration and smacked a fist into his open palm. "I miss the old days. You know, when the worst thing we had to deal with was the citizens of the Drift trying to beat each other senseless every night. Now we've got pharma cartels flooding the place with their poison, a traitor in the ranks, and corporate conspiracies."

"Behold civilization," Dash joked, gesturing around them. The Drift was still a wild, rough place, but Mack was right. It was slowly changing. The war they were fighting today would determine what this place would be in the future.

"I don't know about you, but I could do with a little less civilization right now."

"Then I guess we're going to Nova to have a drink."

Mack nodded. "And if we're lucky, our happily-married brethren will have a few suggestions for us—once they stop laughing."

"As I recall, we laughed at them. Hell, I seem to recall you observing that you'd give love a miss, based on the way it made Kit and Luke act the day they proposed."

"That would be the same day you called them both love-struck and goofy looking," Mack reminded him.

"*Fraxx*, they're really going to enjoy this, aren't they?"

"Uh huh." Mack clapped him on the shoulder. "Might as well get it over with. This is not at all the way I wanted this evening to go. How did we go from having a romantic dinner at home with Lieksa to this?"

"We both know the answer to that. We screwed up. Now, let's go get that drink." There wasn't any point in talking about how they had gotten here. All that mattered was what they were going to do next.

* * * *

"I still think you should have thumped them both a good one before leaving. Maybe it would've knocked some sense into their thick skulls," Cynder declared over their second round of drinks.

Lieksa laughed at the cyborg woman's suggestion. "If I had your strength, then maybe it would have worked. Since I'm an unenhanced, ordinary human, I don't think it would have done anything."

"Might have made you feel better. If you ever want to learn a few moves, let me know. I'd be happy to teach you." Cynder grinned and raised her glass. "We ladies have to look out for each other, right?"

"Right!" Zura agreed, her voice carrying far enough to make several of the other patrons of the VIP section glance their way.

The Nova Club was an interesting place. Part night club, part gambling den, it seemed to have something for everyone, including a fully caged fighting ring with spectator seating. Tonight wasn't a scheduled fight night, but it was still a crowded, bustling place. Zura had met them at the door and escorted them straight to the VIP section, where the music was quieter, and they were away from the press of the crowd.

The view from their table was breathtaking. Nova was located on the outer curve of the station, which meant it had viewports that let the inhabitants look out into space. Stars were scattered across the ink-black sky like diamonds, millions of them, forming a sea of cold light as far as she could see. It was beautiful.

After a lifetime of living inside protective walls, Lieksa rarely thought about what existed outside. This view, like Alyson's projected window, was a reminder that there was more to life than the small world she had created for herself. It was safe and stable inside her little bubble, but it also lacked a few things; like music, friends, laughter…and love.

Alyson gave her a soft nudge. "You okay?"

"Yeah. At least, I will be." She turned her attention to Zura. "Can I ask you something personal?"

Zura's silver eyes widened, and a small smile played across her lips. "You want to know how I deal with being married to a couple of cybernetic former soldiers?"

"Well, yes. I mean, Cynder's cyborg, too, so I imagine it's a little easier, but how do you both manage?"

Cynder laughed and gestured to Zura. "I can't wait to hear this. Spill, Little Blue, how do you manage my big, bossy, batch brothers?"

Zura's blue-striped complexion darkened several shades. "There are times when I like them bossy."

"If this just turned into a sex talk, I'm going to need another drink first. Those are my brothers you're married to," Cynder said.

"It's not the bedroom that's the problem," Lieksa clarified, blushing, too. "It's that they don't seem to be able to stop working. They keep secrets, and Dash has a bad habit of listening in on private conversations. They were eavesdropping the day you asked me to do that favor for you, Alyson. They haven't been intel-gathering assets since the war ended, but they're still acting that way."

All three women were silent for a little while, but eventually, Cynder spoke. "I never knew what they did during the wars. They don't talk about it much. None of us do. You know better than most what it was like for us back then. We all cope with it in our own way. Kit, Luke, and I focused on building this club. Your guys came straight here after they were freed and gave themselves a new mission, to make the Drift a safe place to live."

It made sense, but it wasn't the information Lieksa needed. "I understand needing a mission, a sense of purpose. What I can't make them see is that I have mine, too. They don't want me trying to dig up that information you asked me to find, Alyson. They said it's too dangerous. They're out there every day, risking their lives, but they won't let me make the same choice. I want to help. I *need* to help. I have a lot to make up for, why can't they understand that?"

"What do you think you have to make up for?" Alyson asked, her voice so soft Lieksa could barely hear her over the beat of the music.

"I told you I was a tech for Nobar Tech. It was my job to repair the cyborgs. I patched them up and sent them back into battle. Sometimes we did experimental upgrades. Like what I did to Dash and Mack." Guilt hit her, tearing into her soul with jagged claws. "I thought I was repairing machines. I didn't know. I sent so many of them back into battle to be hurt again, or killed."

"And when you found out the truth?" Alyson coaxed her.

"I stopped. I protected Dash and Mack as best I could, and I walked away. It wasn't enough, though. It won't ever be enough. How many cyborgs died because of me? How much suffering did I cause?"

"*Re'veth*." Cynder set down her glass with a thunk that shook the table. "You didn't kill any of us. You were there to put us back together again, and you did your job. That doesn't make you a killer. You saved Dash's life. You should take credit for saving all our lives. You knew what we were before anyone else did. You knew, and you didn't say a word. You protected us."

"She testified, too. She was one of the ones who made sure the galaxy knew the truth," Alyson said.

Lieksa's head snapped up and she stared at Alyson in shock. "How could you know anything about it? No one knows. If they did, I'd never work for any corporation again."

Alyson winked. "It was an educated guess. When I started treating the cyborgs on the station, I did a lot of research. What you told me about your situation seemed familiar, so I went back and looked at the testimonies. They were all anonymous, but I found one that I thought might be yours. Now I know it was."

"You can't say anything. None of you can. If anyone found out, I'd lose my job, and it would be hard to find another one out here where the corporations run everything."

"They don't run the medical center. I'm not affiliated with any of them, I just lease space." Alyson leaned forward and steepled her hands on the table in front of her. "Come work for me.

You're wasting your talent at Astek. Any tech can repair a droid."

The offer surprised her, but there was no way she could agree to it. "I don't work on living systems anymore."

"You worked on Dash," Zura pointed out.

"If I hadn't, he'd have died."

"That's why I want you to come to the medical center. Dash isn't the only cyborg on the Drift. Far from it. While I can heal physical injuries, I don't know enough about cybernetic implants to help them if they get damaged."

"And what will I do the rest of the time? I'm not a doctor, Alyson. I'm not qualified to work on regular people."

"I've been thinking about that. If your training was as extensive as I think it was, then you should be able to get certified as a medic without much trouble or training time. I can teach you what you need to know, and in exchange, you can teach me more about cyborgs. Someone needs to take care of them."

Cynder nodded. "We go to Alyson because we trust her. Most of us don't trust the corporations. How can we? They've never had our best interests at heart."

"Why would they think I was any different? I worked for the corporations then, and I work for another one, now."

"Well, for one thing, you're dating two cyborgs. That certainly puts you in the pro-cyborg camp," Zura said.

"I don't know what we are right now." And wasn't that the truth.

Cynder snickered. "Trust me, you're dating. Cyborg men are too stubborn to give up that easily. They're probably off somewhere coming up with an apology plan. My guys had to chase me across the damned Drift when I walked out on them. In comparison, your guys have it easy."

"Your guys also had a little help from your brothers and me," Zura reminded her sister-in-law with a grin.

Alyson shook her head. "This is why I don't date. I can't find time in my life for one stubborn, difficult man. I have no idea how you all manage with two each."

"It takes patience, communication—" Zura started speaking, but Cynder cut her off.

"And a lot of hot sex. The sex is key."

"Especially the make-up sex," Zura agreed and drained her glass. "Next round is on me."

Zura left the table to put in their order, her small form quickly getting lost in the sea of patrons.

"You don't have to make up your mind tonight, Lieksa. Take your time and think about it. I would love it if you came to work at the medical center, but only if it's the right fit for you."

"I appreciate the offer, and I will think about it. After I left Nobar, I swore I wouldn't work on living systems anymore, but this would be different. I'd be helping, not hurting."

"Exactly." Alyson looking pleased.

Cynder raised her glass, then stopped. Her expression cooled slightly as she spotted someone or something she didn't like. "I thought he was supposed to be home, recovering."

Alyson glanced up, then sighed. "Why am I not surprised? She gestured for someone to join them, and a moment later, Len appeared at their table, looking slightly abashed.

"This is not what I meant by taking some time to relax, Officer Daniels."

He grinned and shrugged. "Yeah, well, I was bored out of my mind and needed to stretch my legs. My favorite visitor stopped dropping by once you cut me loose." He turned to wink at Lieksa. "I've missed your smile since I got out of medical."

If things had been different, she would have blushed at the way Len was flirting. He was cute, in a boyish way, with an warm smile and friendly manner that made it easy to like him. It didn't matter, though. He wasn't Mack or Dash, and that meant she wasn't interested.

"It's nice to see you up and around, even if you probably shouldn't be, yet. Dr. Jefferies is right, you should be at home, recovering."

"Just came to say hi to a few friends and test my luck at the tables. I managed to survive being shot and avoid getting blown up recently. If my luck holds maybe I can win enough to retire and spend the rest of my days in the lap of luxury."

Cyn snorted. "Luck never holds for long, especially not on the gaming floor."

Len ignored Cynder and leaned in closer to Lieksa. "Speaking of luck, how's Dash doing? You had any luck restoring his memories? I sure would like to know how those bastards got the drop on us. One minute we were good, and the next I'm on the ground wondering what the *fraxx* happened."

"I'm close to a fix. At least, I think I am. I should know by tomorrow if it's going to work." The idea had come to her that morning. The data-mining device she had installed to download information from Astek's systems might be able to pull Dash's missing memories. They should still be encoded somewhere in his processors, it was accessing them that was proving to be a problem. The black-market tech might be the workaround she had been looking for. She had planned on telling them about her idea tonight, but then everything went sideways.

"That's great to hear," Len said.

"With everything that's going on, I know how important it is to recover that data. Speaking of which, are you sure it's safe for you to be out alone? You were targeted once already," she pointed out.

He opened his arms wide and shrugged. "I'm not going to go into hiding. If those cartel bastards want me, they'll find me no matter what. I might as well enjoy myself in the meantime."

"I'm not sure that's the smart play, but I'm not the one with a target on my back." Cynder rose and went to meet Zura, who was on her way back to their table with a tray full of drinks.

"Like I always say, it's better to be lucky than good. Speaking of which, the tables are calling my name. Good evening, ladies." He made an odd gesture with one hand and turned to leave, his other hand brushing across her shoulder as he moved away.

"I don't normally say this about our customers, but that one needs to find a new hobby. For all his talk about luck, he loses far more than he wins," Cynder said as she reappeared with Zura right behind her.

"Len gambles? Lieksa asked, surprised. Then again, she didn't know him very well, and when she thought about it, he'd talked her into playing cards with her every time she visited.

"Every chance he gets. For most people, the gaming tables are entertainment, but not him. Luck is his religion, and this place is his temple." Cynder reclaimed her seat and claimed one of the drinks from the tray. "I was about to make a toast before we were interrupted, and since I believe we're about to be interrupted again, I'll make this quick. "To friends, old and new. We need to get together like this more often."

She tipped back her head and drank, leaving Lieksa to wonder what the next interruption would be. She looked around, but the light was too dim for her to see anything at first. It took a moment for her to spot Mack and Dash on the far side of the room, looking her way.

"They followed me here? Who do they think they are?" she muttered.

"I asked them for space, and they can't even give me that!" Without another word Lieksa downed the contents of her glass and left the table, doing her best to ignore the burn in her throat and the slight weave in her walk as she stomped through the crowd. It was time she set them straight on a few things.

CHAPTER TWELVE

"*Fraxx*, she's not happy to see us." Mack swore as Lieksa left the table and came straight for them, her lovely features marred by an angry frown.

"Which isn't surprising, considering she told us to give her some space." Dash turned to Kit. "You're going to vouch for the fact we didn't know she was here, right?"

The big cyborg rolled his eyes. "If you two hadn't made a habit of spying on her, this wouldn't be a problem."

"One time is not a habit!" Mack protested.

"Is that a note of panic I hear in your voice, Mack?" Luke asked with a snicker. "She's really got you two tied up in knots. That's a good sign. It means she might really be the one."

Mack glanced over at his friend and grunted in irritation. "Of course she's the one. It's always been her. Now, are you two going to stand there and laugh, or help us make this right?"

Kit and Luke stopped laughing. "We'll help. But all you really need to do is repeat what you just said. It worked for Jaeger and Toro, it'll work for you two idiots."

"Did it work for you?" Dash asked.

"We never screwed up this badly. Apparently, we're the smart ones," Luke said.

"Smart, but slow. As I recall, it took you guys months to even ask Zura out."

"I'd argue with you, but I think someone else wants that honor," Kit stepped back and leaned against the bar, leaving room for Lieksa, who marched straight up to Mack and jabbed her finger into his chest.

"Why are you two here? I told you I could take care of myself, and I can. Not that I'd have to right now. I'm with Cynder, and I'm pretty sure she could take down a Nantari rhino without breaking a sweat, but that's beside the point. The point is…" She frowned. "The point is, you two need to stop following me."

"We're here to talk to Luke and Kit about a few things. We didn't follow you. We didn't know you were here until we walked through that door and saw you with your friends."

"Kit and Luke can vouch for us. Right, guys?" Dash prompted.

"They asked if they could drop by and talk. They've been hanging out with us in the back for over an hour." Kit said.

Lieksa sighed. "Okay. And you're not going to follow me now, right?"

"Not unless you ask us to, sweetheart."

"Not going to happen. You can keep your charming charms to yourself, mister spy guy."

Luke snickered. "Mister spy guy is now your new nickname, Dash. Better get used to it."

"Not helping, Luke."

"Just paying back an old debt. Did you think I'd forgotten what happened the day we proposed to Zura?"

"I was hoping you had, yeah."

Lieksa glowered at Luke and shook a finger in his direction. "You hush."

Luke wisely kept his mouth closed and moved back the same time Kit did, leaving them alone at the bar.

"You're sexy as hell when you're sassy. Especially when you're not sassing us," Dash said.

"You're incredible no matter what you're doing. Since we're all here, do you want to talk about things?" Mack asked her and offered her his hand. He wanted to fold her into his arms and hold her until she softened, but he couldn't risk it. Being overprotective and pushy was what had them in this situation in the first place.

When she took his hand, a warm glow settled into his chest and wrapped around his heart.

"I'm still not ready for that. We said we'd talk tomorrow. Can we still do that?"

He squeezed her fingers gently. "Call us when you're ready to talk, and we'll be there."

"I will."

She gifted them both with a tiny smile that made him want to slay dragons in her name.

Dash spoke. "Before you go back to your friends, I need to ask you something. When you were talking to Len, he said something and then made a gesture with his fingers, sort of like he was pulling a trigger. Do you remember what he said to you?"

She snatched her hand out of Mack's grasp and stepped back, glowering at Dash with distrust. "You *were* spying on me!"

"If I were, I wouldn't have to ask you what he said, would I? There was something familiar about the gesture, that's all. I've seen it before, but I don't know where." Dash raised his hands in a placating gesture.

Lieksa stopped moving away, but her expression was guarded and her tone was wary. "He said something about it being better to be lucky than good. Then, after he was gone, Cynder mentioned he's obsessed with luck and gambles a lot. Maybe you heard him say it around the squad room?"

"Maybe. I don't know. Something about it seemed important." Dash shook his head as if the action could somehow dislodge the information he was looking for.

"Remember what the doctor said—the memories are more likely to come if you don't force it. Whatever it was, I'm sure it'll come back to you eventually. I'm going now. I'll talk to you tomorrow."

After she was out of earshot, Mack turned on Dash. "What the hell was that about? You nearly screwed us up all over again."

"I'm not sure. Something about the gesture made me think about the day I got shot. There's something about it. Something I need to remember." Dash groaned and pinched the bridge of his nose with fingers. He hated the idea of leaving Lieksa again, but she needed more time, and the Nova Club was the safest place in the galaxy for her right now. If anyone dangerous came near her, Cynder would take them apart, and Zura would stomp on the pieces.

* * * *

Lieksa wasn't happy she had walked away from Mack and Dash again. There was an ache in her chest no amount of alcohol was going to ease. She wanted to be with them, but if she turned around now, she would end up going home with them. It would be too easy to stop being angry and let it go, but that wouldn't solve anything, and she loved them too much to take the easy way out.

She nearly tripped over her own feet as that last thought bounced around her brain a few more times. *Re'veth*. She loved them.

"Then I guess I better figure out a way to make this work," she muttered to herself as she made her way through the crowd.

As she passed into the VIP section, her comm device started to vibrate and chirp an alert sequence. For a moment she had no idea what it could be about, and she fumbled several times getting the thing out of her pocket. A quick scan of the readout jogged her memory, and she slipped the device back into her pocket. Her little spy-bot was reporting in. It had found something and was headed back to her workshop.

Once back at the table, she gave Alyson a hug from behind. "You remember that favor you asked me for the other day? It looks like I might have found something for you. I need go check it out, though. Right now."

Alyson put her hand over Lieksa's forearm and squeezed. "Everything okay with the guys? Do you want me to go with you?"

"The guys are fine. They were here for the same reason I was. Drinks with friends. We're going to talk tomorrow."

"That's good."

"Dash said he remembered something. It wasn't much, but he was pushing himself again. Maybe you could check in on him?"

"You'll be careful, right?" Alyson asked.

"Very. I'll message you as soon as I know anything."

"And when you get home, too. "

She rolled her eyes and laughed. "Yes, mom."

The others weren't eager to let her go, but once she hinted at where she was going, they stopped protesting. A quick round of hugs and a promise to get together again soon and she was on her way. Cynder walked her to a private exit at the back of the club, saving her another trip through the jostling crowd. When Cyn walked outside with her, Lieksa tried to protest, but her argument fell on deaf ears.

"I'm walking with you. If anything happened to you, I'd never forgive myself, and neither would Mack or Dash."

She made the trip to Astek headquarters with a bounce in her step and a smile. It had been far too long since she had a girls' night out, no matter what events had made it necessary. It was nice of Cynder to walk with her, even if Lieksa still didn't really believe it was necessary.

They parted company at the front door. Cynder headed back to her bar, while Lieksa made her way through security and down to her workshop. Once there, she removed the black-market tech from the maintenance bot and sent the robot on its way again, making sure there was nothing in its logs to give away where it had been or what it had been doing. The tech should be undetectable, but why take chances? If anyone noticed the breach, she wasn't going to make it easy for them to figure out how it had been done, or by whom.

Once the bot was gone, she uploaded the stolen data to her tablet and started scrolling through it, looking for anything that might be helpful.

It didn't take long for her to find what she was looking for. The files were from a server on the executive floors, protected by firewalls and security systems that should have kept them safe from ever being discovered. Whoever had stored them there had been so certain of their security they hadn't even bothered to encrypt them.

By the time she was finished scanning it all, Lieksa would never work for any corporation again. How could she? They had made a choice to intentionally inject every cyborg woman with a substance that would render her incapable of having children. There was an antidote, but it had never been manufactured. It only existed as a formula buried in a database. The bastards never had any intention of reversing what they had done.

There was too much data for her to read in one sitting. It would take hours for her and Alyson to review and make sense of it all. Much of what she saw was couched in medical and technical doublespeak, but she'd read more than her share of those types of reports when she worked for Nobar Tech. She had even written a few.

She saved a copy of the data to her tablet, encrypted it, detached the widget, and slipped it into her pocket. Once she was home, she would make more copies of the files and make sure that enough people had them that there was no chance that the corporations could track them all down. She wouldn't let this genie get shoved back in its bottle. The people who had done this needed to answer for what they had done.

She typed out a brief message on her comm device and sent it to Alyson, along with an encrypted copy of the file. "Found the book I told you about. I hope you enjoy reading it. Headed home soon."

After that was done, Lieksa leaned against her workbench and looked around the cluttered room she'd spent most of her waking hours in since coming to Astek Station. It was time to move on. She wouldn't miss the place, or the work. She would miss Zale, but once he forgave her for quitting on him, she hoped they could still be friends. Despite his tendency to bellow like a wounded bear, he had been a good boss.

To keep up appearances, she would have to come in to work tomorrow and give proper notice, but this was goodbye. She wandered around the cramped space one last time, breathing in the familiar scents of grease and burned-out circuit boards. She was still lost in her moment of farewell when she heard the distinctive sound of a door opening. *Fraxx.* Who was down here with her? All the warnings Mack and Dash had given her over the last few days had her pulse racing as she looked around for something she could use as a weapon.

"Hello?"

A familiar bellow shook the walls of her workshop. "That better be you in there, Lieksa, or I'm going to have to kick someone's ass!"

"It's me, Zale. What are you doing here at this hour?" she asked, relief coursing through her. Of course it was her boss. They were both notorious for working late hours.

Her boss appeared in the doorway, a hand on the firearm at his hip and wearing a smile broad enough to show a flash of his fangs. "I'm here to find out who tripped my security alarm. Care to explain what you're doing rattling around so late? I thought you went home hours ago. Hot date and all that."

"Hot date went cold so I came here to do some work, and some thinking. Sorry I made you come down here. I didn't know you'd upped the security protocols."

He entered the workshop and joined her at the far end. "With everything going on around the station right now, I thought a little extra security couldn't hurt. I only left a little while ago, so it was no problem coming back. Do I need to have a word with those men of yours? I'm sure I warned you not to get involved with those two."

"You can have a word with them after I do. We're working through a few things. I guess I'm working through a few things, myself."

"You okay? You look like you've got something on your mind. I'm a neutral party, if you feel like talking."

That made her laugh. Zale wasn't even close to being neutral. He had her back from the first day she started to work here. Until recently, he was her only friend on the station.

"Remember the day Dash got hurt? You and I had a conversation about secrets and punishing ourselves," she asked.

He nodded. "I remember. My offer still stands. You tell me yours, I'll tell you mine."

She blew out a soft breath and decided to trust her instincts. He deserved to know why she was leaving.

"You were right. I was doing penance down here. During the Resource Wars, I worked for Nobar Tech. I was assigned to a hospital ship, and it was my job to repair their cyborgs and send them back into battle. Sometimes I conducted experimental upgrades, too. I thought I was working on machines, but then one day two of my charges refused a direct order. Instead of letting go of me, one of them kissed me. They told me the truth about who, and what they really were. I quit the next day, and I never knew what happened to the men who entrusted me with their secret. Not until you sent me to repair one of them."

His pure black eyes widened. "No way. That's why things between the three of you heated up so fast?"

"Yeah. I thought they died in the war. They thought the same about me. You know how it was back then. Hostile takeovers, data being deliberately wiped, servers destroyed. We all moved on, and then the tech who filled their heads with experimental hardware and abandoned them suddenly reappears. It's been a little intense."

Low rumbles of laughter filled the workshop. "You always did have a talent for understatement. They were the reason you swore not to work on another living system, huh? You felt guilty about what you'd done to them."

"I did. Today, Dr. Jefferies offered me a job at her medical center. She wants me to work on the cyborgs with her. She'll teach me what I need to know to be a medic, and I'll teach her about cybernetic implants and medi-bots."

Zale sighed. "I always knew you had too much talent to stay for long. This means I'll have to break in yet another tech who is going to hate the job and get buried under the workload within a week or two. *Fraxx*, you have no idea how much I'm going to miss you."

"I think that's the nicest thing you've ever said to me."

He shrugged. "I was never good at motivating employees with kindness. Bellowing and intimidation always worked better."

She reached out to swat his arm playfully. "You're really not that intimidating."

He growled and flashed his fangs. "Hey! No reason to be insulting. Especially when you still haven't told me the real reason why you were down here."

"I did. I told you, I was thinking."

"Uh huh. What part of your cognitive process required a cleaner bot arriving outside your workshop door less than twenty minutes before you did?" He made a show of looking around. "I don't see one around here, anywhere, but my security logged one. Funny thing, it wasn't programmed to clean this level."

Fraxx. "You're better off not knowing," she said, hoping that he'd leave it alone.

"Probably. That isn't going to stop me from asking again."

Zale folded his arms across his massive chest, and she could swear he settled deeper into his stance. He looked determined enough to withstand being rammed by a battle cruiser. Clearly, she wasn't getting out of here without telling him the truth, or at least part of it.

"I was looking for information on the cyborgs. Something was done to them before they were released, and I was hoping I could find out more about what was done, and how to reverse it."

"And did you find it? Judging by your solemn expression when I came in, I'm betting you did. You're right. I'd be better off not knowing any of this. Since it's too late for that, why don't you tell me what you found."

"The corporations made the female cyborgs infertile before releasing them. All of them, Zale. They can't have children unless they're given some kind of antidote, and so far, Dr. Jeffries hasn't been able to pin down exactly what they were given, never mind how to reverse it. Tonight I managed to find the files that show what was done, and how to undo it."

Instead of looking surprised, Zale nodded. "I told them it was only a matter of time before someone figured it out. They didn't listen, obviously. They were still thinking about the cyborgs as machines, not human beings, when they made that decision.

"I told you if you shared your secrets, I'd share mine. It's my turn for confession." Zale relaxed some, leaning his big bulk up against the worktable, which shifted slightly beneath his weight. "I've worked for Astek a long time. More than a decade, now. My specialty was nanotech. I designed the medi-bots that kept their organic elements functional." He winced. "I hate it when the old terms creep in. Organic elements. Like they weren't living beings at all. Just machines with organic bits tacked on."

"I know." She reached out and placed her hand on his arm. It was easy to forget that she wasn't the only one who felt guilty about what they'd done during the wars. Everyone who was part of the war had to come to terms with the revelation the cyborgs weren't machines, and some of them had suffered at the hands of people who hadn't know better.

"You might want to save your sympathy until the end of my story. I'm not sure I deserve it."

She left her hand on Zale's arm. "I just confessed to stealing data from our employer. I promise you, I'm in no place to be judging anyone."

"I know all about what's in those files. When the war ended, and the victors were finished picking over the carcasses of their enemies, they had to decide what to do with the cyborgs. Their neat, tidy, *bloodless* war and humane disposal plans all went to hell when the cyborgs made it known they weren't machines at all. They had to release their creations, but the corporations couldn't risk letting the medi-bots finding their way into the human population. If any of the women got pregnant, there was a ninety-seven percent chance that their medi-bots would bond with the fetus and become part of them. Meaning any children they had would be born with nanotech we couldn't remove or deactivate. The men could reproduce without a problem, but the women..." He sighed and shook his head.

"That's when I got involved. They wanted a way to permanently block fertility, but it had to be something subtle, and it had to be something the medi-bots couldn't detect, or they'd filter it out. Everyone on the team voiced some level of concern about the plan. It didn't sit right with us, but orders were orders, and there were some pretty grim alternatives on the table if we didn't come up with something."

"You did that to them? Ended any hope of them ever having a family?"

"It was better than sentencing them to death. Believe me, there were some very powerful people who thought that was the way to go. It was the lesser evil. That doesn't make it any easier for me to sleep at night, but it's the truth."

"Didn't you want to tell someone?"

"Of course I did. Every *fraxxing* day. But I signed some scary non-disclosure agreements. The kind that meant if I whispered a word to anyone they'd lock me away, along with everyone I cared about. My cousin works for Astek, too. He designs artificial intelligence programs. I got him the damned job. What do you think would happen to him if I spoke out?"

"I understand." Fear of retribution was the reason she had testified anonymously. She couldn't blame Zale for making the same choices she had. The question was, what choice would he make now? Would he let her walk out of here with the data?

"Were you going to take those files to the doctor so she could undo what was done?"

"That was the plan, yeah."

"Do you understand that if you do that, there will be repercussions? The ones who made this happen are still out there, and they've got a vested interest in keeping this quiet."

She nodded. From the moment she had agreed to Alyson's request to help, she had known there would be risks. "I'm done keeping secrets. That doesn't mean I'm going to rush to announce what I've done. It'll take time for Alyson to create an antidote, and even after she has it, I don't expect every cyborg woman in the galaxy to suddenly decide she wants a baby. There are going to be a lot of risks involved, for everyone. Including you—if you let me walk out of here with that." She nodded toward her data tablet, still sitting on the workbench.

Zale glanced at the tablet, then reached over and pushed it toward her. "I'm not going to stop you. This might be the only chance I get to make things right. I'd like to sleep through the night again someday, you know?"

She knew exactly what he meant. "Thank you." She threw her arms around him in a bear hug. He was taking a huge risk. They both knew it.

He hugged her back. "Tomorrow you need to come into work like it was a normal day. You can hand in your notice, I'll bitch and complain and send you off to your new job with my boot print on your ass, exactly the same way I treated the three techs who quit this job before you."

"You got it. You know you're not going to be rid of me that easily, right? You still owe me the drink you promised me if I passed my probation period. You can come by the Nova Club or Amped one night and pay up."

"You want a drink from me, I'll buy you a round at the Nova. Amped is a little too rich for my blood. And given that you never seem to go anywhere besides here or your cubby, I'm a little surprised you even suggested the place."

She grinned. "As it happens, Mack and Dash are friends with the owners of both places. They've been expanding my horizons."

"I'll just bet they have," Zale chuckled and released her from their hug. "They know what you're doing down here?"

She grunted noncommittally. "Yes and no."

"I take it they don't approve?"

"Not really. They're worried I'm going to get hurt. Between the lunatic trying to wipe out the taskforce they lead and my extracurricular activities, they're convinced I need to be protected from the world day and night. I'm not some delicate Tiskalian ice orchid. I won't wilt and die the first time someone breathes on me."

"No, you're tougher than that, but no one's tough enough to survive an explosion or a shot to the head at close range. Well, no one but your boyfriend. Why don't you let me walk you home? Make sure you, and everything you're carrying gets there safe and sound."

Her first instinct was to say no, but she needed to stop doing that. She *was* a target, and she had already taken enough risks with the data currently in her possession. She needed to get home and disseminate copies of the files to the others.

"Thank you, Zale."

Tomorrow, she was going to have to apologize to Dash and Mack, too. She hadn't been entirely reasonable with them. They still needed to stop treating her like she was made of glass, but it was time she admitted her share of the blame in this whole mess. Then she could tell them what she'd discovered, which was likely going to make them both even more overprotective.

"I'll wipe the security log once we're out of here, too. It will be like the bot was never here, and none of this conversation ever happened."

"Sounds like a plan." If only the rest of her life could be fixed so easily. There was no do-over button for reality. If there were, she would have punched it years ago, and gotten back all the time she'd lost with Dash and Mack. Out of all the regrets she had in her life, past and present, the years they had spent apart were at the top of her list.

Even if everything worked out for them in the future, they wouldn't be together forever. No one knew how long the cyborgs would live, but their medi-bots made it likely their lifespans would far outlast any normal human's. They were going to outlive her by decades, if not centuries, which meant every day they'd lost was that much more precious.

Going forward, she was going to do her best to make sure there weren't any more lost days to regret.

CHAPTER THIRTEEN

Dash was fighting to remember, but it was like trying to catch hold of a wisp of smoke.

He paced the length of one of the private rooms in the back of the Nova Club, while Mack sat on a nearby couch, watching with concern. He had tried offering up suggestions at first, but after Dash shot down every one of them, he had wisely opted for silence.

There was something about the gesture Len had made when he was speaking to Lieksa. He couldn't shake the feeling it was important. The second he saw it, his pulse had kicked up a few beats per second and and his shoulder ached where he'd been shot. There was no way that was a coincidence. His subconscious was trying to tell him something.

He went round and round inside his head, chasing after-echoes of a memory until he couldn't think straight. "*Fraxx*! I hate this. How do humans deal with such limited memory capacity?"

"They've never had perfect recall. You can't miss what you've never experienced."

"Insightful, but not very helpful right now," he snapped.

"If you want, I could try hitting you upside the head. Maybe that would help."

"I'm pretty sure that's not a medically sound approach to memory retrieval, asshole."

"Probably not, but I'm here for you, my friend. Whatever it takes."

A knock at the door cut off his reply. Since they were still at the club, there weren't many people it could be, and all of them were owners with more right to be there than either he or Mack. He called out, loud enough to be heard through the metal door. "You don't have to knock, you know. You do own the place."

The door slid open, revealing their visitor to be someone unexpected. "As much fun as that would be, I don't have time to run a bar. I have all these patients, you see. Some of whom are really lousy at taking my advice."

"I thought you were off the clock," Mack said to Alyson.

"I was, but Lieksa asked me to look in on Dash. She said you were struggling to remember something. Funny thing, I distinctly remember telling you not to force things. Your brain will heal at its own pace, Dash."

"I don't have the luxury of time, Doc. I need to remember. Now. Something I saw tonight triggered a memory, but I can't quite pin it down. It's important that I do."

"Then sit down and let me try something. I don't promise it will work, but it has a better shot at working than your current technique of pacing a hole in the deck-plating and beating yourself up." Alyson pointed to an empty couch. "Sit."

"Has anyone told you that you have the bedside manner of a Terran pit bull?" he asked as he took a seat exactly where she'd pointed. One thing he had learned while under Alyson's care was that she would put up with a fair bit of backtalk, but only if it was accompanied by compliance.

"That's a kind of canine, isn't it? Do you really think now's a good time to be insulting me?" She took a seat beside him.

"I tried flirting with you, once. As I recall, that didn't go so well, either." The only woman he planned on flirting with from now on was their red-headed angel of mercy. Somehow, they were going to get past everything. They had to. The universe hadn't brought the three of them together just to tear them apart again. He couldn't believe that.

"You ever spy on either one of us again, she might shoot you herself. Then who's going to put you back together?" Alyson asked with a hint of a smile. "Now, close your eyes and get comfortable. This might take a while."

Mack cleared his throat. "Anything I can do?"

"If he doesn't stay still, you have my permission to restrain him. Otherwise, you're fine where you are."

Dash cracked open an eye. "I don't remember you being this bloodthirsty."

"You upset my friend. More than that, you hurt her. That's a conversation from another time, however. I need you to be relaxed for this process to have any shot at working, and from what I've seen, your love life is not exactly a tranquil topic.

Okay, Dash, I want you to keep your eyes closed and try to relax. I'm going to talk you through a short breathing exercise to help with that."

"I'm ready." He did as he was told, inhaling and exhaling according to the calmly spoken instructions Alyson gave him. It wasn't easy to stop thinking about things at first, but eventually, she declared him ready for the next step.

"Think back to the day you were wounded. Find the last complete memory you have of that day, and tell me about it. Try to use your real memory as much as you can. I know there's going to be some overlap."

Dash took a deep breath and thought back to the day of the raid. It was an inaccurate, messy process, but he got there eventually. It would have been far quicker to use his enhanced memory bank, but the doctor was right, that wasn't going help him remember anything.

"We're outside the main doors. Mack's going over our assignments one last time. Movements. Targets. Goals. The team is restless. They want to get going. We've been planning this for more than a week. Everyone knows what they're supposed to do."

"They're restless. How about you, Dash. How are you feeling?" Alyson asked.

"Adrenaline's pumping. I'm on edge. Sharp and ready to go. Mack's still talking, though. Reminding Len—Officer Daniels—his new assignment is to keep me in one piece." Dash chuckled. "I'd forgotten about that. Guess he didn't obey that order, huh, Mack?"

"He was wounded trying to follow those orders, so I think we'll give him a pass," Alyson said. "What else do you remember?"

"The door breach went perfectly. We go in. There should have been a deal going down, but the place appears empty. The team moves to their positions. I head for the stairs that lead up to the catwalk. My job is to get eyes on the whole area so I can send the data back to Mack. Len goes first. I follow. We make it about halfway up before anything else happens. This is where it starts to go fuzzy."

"Stay in the moment, Dash. Think about what you can see and hear. Is there a smell? A sound? Where are you right now?"

"Metal. There's cold metal under my hand." He focused on the small details, and the memory grew clearer. "I'm on the ladder. We're nearly to the catwalk. Len is above me. There's a crash. Crates! I remember the crates being toppled. They're blocking the door. Our primary exit is blocked. There's comm chatter about it. Teams reporting in. A few more seconds and I'll be in position. Len's made it to the top. Once I join him, I'll create the link between Mack and I, and—It was Len. Son of a starbeast, Len's the one that shot me." His memory was still imperfect, but he remembered enough to know what had happened. He climbed onto the catwalk, expecting Len to be in position already. Instead, his partner had a firearm pointed at his head.

"I always said it's better to be lucky than good. Sorry, Dash. Today's not going to be your lucky day." He'd made that trigger pulling gesture with his off-hand and then opened fire.

His cyborg reflexes had saved his life. In the split second before the weapon fired, he charged at Len. The sudden change of position was enough to cause the first shot to hit his shoulder instead of blowing his face off. He remembered grappling with Len, but that was when his memory ended. The next thing he remembered was waking up in the medical center. It didn't matter, though. What he did recall was more than enough.

His eyes snapped open, and he launched himself off the couch. "We need to find Len, now!"

Mack was already on his comm device. "Kit. We need you to locate Len Daniels. He was in the bar a little while ago. If he's still there, let us know but do not approach. And tell Cynder she needs to bring Lieksa somewhere safe. Quickly and without raising suspicion."

"Lieksa's not here. She left a few minutes after she talked to the two of you," Alyson said, her voice thick with worry.

"Where did she go? And what did Len say to her?" Dash's heart was hammering a staccato beat against his ribs, and his stomach was full of bitter bile as he tried to come to terms with the fact that a friend had tried to murder him.

"He was asking about you. He wanted to know if she had come up with a way to restore your memory." Alyson's cheeks blanched, and she uttered a low, horrified moan. "She told him she might have thought of a way, and she'd know more tomorrow. Then she went to her workshop."

"If he thinks she can repair my memory, he'll go after her, tonight. The only reason I'm still alive right now is because he didn't think I'd ever remember what happened. "

Mack grunted. "And because you and I left early that day and weren't there when the bomb went off. "

Dash pulled out his comm device. "I'm calling her right now."

Lieksa answered quickly, but her tone was ice cold and her expression stormy as she stared at the screen of her comms. "What do you want now?"

"I need you to tell me where you are, angel. Are you alone?"

"I'm on my way home, and Zale is with me."

"Get home as quickly as you can and stay there. I need you to stay calm and not show any expression change, okay. Someone might be watching you right now. Len Daniels is the leak. He's the one who shot me. You told him you were close to helping me, so it's likely he's going to be coming after you tonight."

"This night keeps getting better," she muttered, but her expression didn't change.

"One of us will be there soon. Okay? We're not going to let anything happen to you."

She flashed him a brief smile, but her eyes were dark with worry. "Don't let anything happen to you, either."

"Send one of us a message once you're safe. And tell Zale to keep his eyes open."

"I will."

Once he ended the communication with her, several things happened at once. Mack heard from Kit, who confirmed that Len wasn't anywhere inside the Nova Club. Alyson checked her messages and found the one Lieksa sent regarding the recovered data, and relayed the find to them.

"So, right now our girlfriend is wandering the station with stolen data in her pocket and a killer on her trail." Mack slammed his fist into a wall. "I'm going after Lieksa. Dash, you get to hunt down the asshole that shot you. Don't let him do it again."

"Don't let him get near our girl."

Mack nodded and vanished into the crowd, leaving Dash to start organizing the hunt for their teammate turned traitor and whoever was helping him. Someone killed Steven Crews and his wife while Len was still laid up in the med center, so he wasn't working alone. Whoever it was, they were probably the ones who had killed their informants, too.

Dash continued contacting the team members still on the station and directed them to meet up at Corp-Sec headquarters. They'd have to take over one of the briefing rooms as a makeshift command center. Not that they were going to be there long. As soon as they had a list of places to hit, they were going to hunt Len down and bring him to justice before he could hurt anyone else.

* * * *

Mack didn't often make use of Corp-Sec's fleet of private transports, but tonight was an exception. He had to get to Lieksa as quickly as possible. He called for a pod to pick him up outside the club, and within minutes he was on his way. He tried to use the travel time to get a handle on his anger, but that wasn't realistic. It would take a trip across the *fraxxing* galaxy and back before he'd be anywhere close to calm.

He was on high alert the entire trip, and the moment he stepped out of the pod, he had his hand on his firearm as he scanned the area.

He made the last leg of the trip on foot. Along the way, he passed Zale, who strolled along as if he didn't have a concern in the world. They didn't speak, but the half-Torski gave him a slight nod as he passed by. When this was over, Mack was going to buy that man a drink or six in appreciation.

The area around her doorway was completely clear. He activated the door chime and smiled when his comm device buzzed a few seconds later. It was Lieksa.

"Please tell me that's you at my door right now," she said in hushed tones.

"It's me. You can let me in, there's no one around."

The door opened, and he was pleased to note she stayed off to one side and out of sight until the door sealed again behind him.

"Cubby, seal door. Security setting maximum," she spoke aloud, and the in-house AI beeped in acknowledgment of her order. "We should be safe, now."

"I'm going to add some additional security measures in a second, but first, I need to do this. You can add it to the list of things I need to apologize for later." With that, he hauled her into his arms and covered her mouth with his.

She melted into his embrace with a sexy little sigh, her arms reaching up to twine around his neck. He pulled her in tight to his body, loving the way her body fit against his. He'd been a fool to distance himself from the one person who made him feel whole.

"I love you," he whispered against her lips.

"I love you, too, you big jerk."

"I deserve that. I will never listen in on your conversations again."

"What about bossing me around all the time?"

"That's never going to change. Being a pushy pain in the ass is part of my programming. I can promise you I'll tell you why I want you to do something, and I will try to listen better. And no more making plans without including you."

"I can work with that. So long as you accept that sometimes, I'm not going to do what you tell me, no matter how much you explain it."

"I can work with that," he repeated her words, and when her eyes lit up, he knew everything would be alright. They'd make this work. They had to, because he wasn't letting her go again.

"Okay then. Why am I hiding in my home with the doors double locked? Where's Dash? What's going on? Oh, and I should tell you that I've got the cure to Cynder and the other cyborg women's infertility on a data stick in my pocket."

"Do you realize how much trouble you're going to be in if they find out you've got hold of that?"

"They're not going to find out. I'll tell you all about that after you tell me about Len. I cannot believe he is the leak…and a killer."

With one last brush of his lips over hers, he let her go and turned his attention to the panel that controlled the door. Her simple security system had worried him since the first time he had seen where she lived, and he had spent some time looking up ways to improve it. There wasn't much to be done, but he did know how to ensure no one used an override command to bypass the locks.

By the time he was finished, he had filled her in on what Dash remembered and what the plan was. Not that it was much of a plan. Hunt the bastard down and protect his most likely target: Lieksa. Dash was already meeting with the rest of the team and anyone else at Corp-Sec he could draft into temporary service.

There were tears in Lieksa's eyes when he finished speaking, and she dashed them away with the back of a shaking hand. "I'm not crying because I'm sad. I'm furious. How could he do that? I trusted him. I *liked* him! All those times he was talking to me, I thought he really cared about Dash, but he was only trying to get information. He used me."

Mack lifted her into his arms and carried her over to the bed, talking all the while. "He used all of us. Len's been on the *crimson* task force since it was formed. We don't know if he was already working for the cartel when he came in, or if they got to him later. Everything we've done from the beginning has been compromised."

He settled on the bed with care, ensuring it was going to take their combined weight before relaxing enough to settle her into his lap. She nuzzled into the crook of his neck, the silken glide of her lips over bare skin igniting needs and desires he did his best to ignore.

"Do you think we'll fit?" she asked.

He was so distracted by his body's response to her touch that it took a few seconds to puzzle out what she meant. When he finally figured it out, his cock turned to stone, and lust poured through him like molten steel.

"Now?" His voice was little more than a gravelly whisper.

"We've lost enough time already, haven't we? I don't want to waste anymore. No more secrets, and no regrets."

CHAPTER FOURTEEN

After everything she had been through today, being in Mack's arms felt like bliss. From their first kiss, he had the power to banish the rest of the world with a touch. Right now, she needed that, and so did Mack. He was here, guarding her instead of watching Dash's back.

"Tell me you love me again," she whispered.

"I love you, Lieksa Kiv. I think I've loved you since the first time I woke up and saw you standing over me with this concerned look on your face. You were gentle and caring, and so *fraxxing* beautiful there was a moment when I thought I'd died and you were an angel sent to greet me."

"I'm no angel," she argued as she started undressing as best she could while curled up in his lap.

"You're our angel," he reminded her, then slanted his mouth across hers.

She parted her lips, inviting him to take the kiss deeper and a low groan rumbled deep in his chest as his tongue swept into her mouth. Need erupted like a solar flare, and she let it consume her.

He palmed her breasts through her shirt, then gripped the fabric in his hands and tore it away, baring her chest as the tattered shreds fell to the floor.

"In a hurry?" she asked as she glanced down at the remains of her shirt.

"Yes, I am. It's been too long since I had you naked and all to myself."

She laughed. "And whose fault is that?"

His eyes were blazing with heat as he lifted his gaze to meet hers. "I should have been with you and Dash the day of the explosion instead of staying at the office. I was determined to find the leak and end the danger to everyone. I didn't think I deserved to spend time with you, enjoying myself when the one who shot Dash was still out there. I was punishing myself, and it never occurred to me that I was punishing you, too. I'm sorry."

"I wasn't sure I deserved to be happy. Not after what I'd done to you and all the other cyborgs I worked on. That's why I agreed to try and dig up information on what was done to Cynder and the female cyborgs. I know you thought I was taking risks I shouldn't, but I wanted to do this. I needed to do something to balance the scales."

"As Dash recently reminded me, neither one of us is responsible for everything that goes wrong in the universe. Maybe we should assign him the permanent duty of pointing that out to you and me from now on."

"Permanent duty?" she repeated his words as hope surged in her breast.

"I love you. I don't see that ever changing, so yeah. This is going to be a permanent thing, isn't it?"

"I love you both, so I guess that means you can have me for as long as you want me," she said.

"Then you best plan on being with us forever, because that's how long I'm going to want you in my life."

"Forever sounds good to me."

"Good. Later, we'll talk about that, and about what you found at Astek, but right now I need you. I know the timing is insane and this bed is too *fraxxing* small, but we'll find a way."

She nodded and rose from his lap, laughing all the while. "We will."

She removed the data stick from her pocket and set it on a narrow shelf above the bed before stripping off the rest of her clothes. Mack wasn't the only one in need right now. After all the hurt, confusion, and stress of the last few days, she needed this, too.

Once she was naked, she stayed where she was and watched Mack shed his clothes. She loved watching the glide and play of muscles under his skin, and her fingers itched to trace the treasure trail of dark hairs that led from his chest down to the waistband of his pants and the thick cock she knew was trapped behind the fabric.

A wicked idea popped into her head, and she stepped in front of him, putting herself between Mack and the bed. She dropped to her knees and grabbed his pants, tugging them down to free his dick. She wasn't waiting for him to take charge. Not this time.

She didn't bother undressing him completely. The second his cock sprang free she leaned in and took the tip into her mouth. His fingers speared into her hair, and he uttered a low groan.

"*Fraxx*, that's good. Your mouth is so hot.

She took him deeper, humming softly as her tongue flicked over his slit and then down the underside of his shaft. When she hit the sensitive spot beneath his glans, he groaned again, his hands tightening his grip on her hair.

"You could do this to me every day of my life, and I will never get tired of it."

She managed a muffled chuckle as she worked his cock with her lips and tongue, pleasuring him as she eased him out of the last of his clothes.

Between them, they managed to get him stripped without mishap, though they both laughed more than once. His pants were still bunched around one ankle when she leaned in and took him to the back of her throat, cupping his sac in her hand at the same time.

He bucked his hips and threw back his head. "If you keep doing that, I'm going to come."

In response, she hollowed her cheeks, increasing the suction until he groaned her name. His cock swelled and jerked in her mouth, and she worked her tongue back and forth across the sensitive tip, determined to push him to the edge of his control.

When he came, it was on a ragged cry of her name, and he emptied himself into her mouth with sharp, jerky thrusts. She released him and tipped her head back to grin at him. "All mine," she declared.

Mack's blood was still sizzling with the force of the orgasm he'd had, but he needed Lieksa under him. He tumbled her onto her narrow bed, barely giving her time to stretch out on the thin mattress before he joined her.

He kissed his way down her body, worshipping every soft inch of her that he could reach as he made his way down to her pussy. She was wet and ready for him, the proof of her need glistening on her inner thighs. He managed to move between her legs, his feet hanging off the edge of the bed as he settled into position. The sweet perfume of her arousal washed over him and he dove in, craving the taste of her.

He wanted to feel her come on his face before he drove his cock into her hot pussy and fucked her the way both of them needed. He licked and sucked with every inch of skill he possessed, determined to break her the way she'd broken him only moments before.

He slid a finger inside, testing her and teasing her at the same time. She arched her hips and took him deeper, gripping the sheets tight as she ground her pussy against his mouth. Their lovemaking grew frenzied and wild, every touch adding to the fire burning between them until she was trembling on the brink of orgasm and his cock was hard and aching, ready to claim what was his.

"I want to watch you come. Now." He uttered the command, and her body obeyed even as she opened her mouth to argue with him. He slipped a second finger into her passage and pressed his thumb against her swollen clit, urging her up and over the edge of her control and into the pleasures that lay behind. She arched her hips off the bed and began to tremble, her breath coming in ragged gasps.

She came with shuddering cry, pulsing around his fingers as she found her release. There was nothing sexier in the worlds than watching her come undone like this. He moved over her still-trembling body and settled himself above her so he could watch her expression as their bodies became one.

"Love you," she whispered as she stroked her hands up his chest to his shoulders and opened her body to him, with a smile that melted his heart.

"Mine," he uttered the single syllable with a groan before driving his cock deep into her welcoming heat.

"Yours," she agreed, her body rising up to meet his.

Time slowed until every second felt like an exquisite hour of bliss and the world beyond the two of them ceased to exist. Her nails scored his skin, the brief bite of pain only adding to the depth of his pleasure. Every glide and thrust brought them closer. Soon he was lost to everything but the slide of sweat-slicked skin, the sweet touch of her lips, and the heat of her body sheathing his.

When she neared the end, her inner walls clamped around him, gripping in a silken vice that turned the smallest movement into a pleasurable torment. His pace quickened, his breath coming in ragged gasps as his control failed and his thrusts grew wilder and more erratic.

She wrapped her legs around his waist and clung to him, riding him as he hit his peak and took her with him. They both cried out at the same time, their bodies locked together as he emptied himself inside her.

When his senses returned she was staring up at him, her blue eyes glowing with happiness and her glorious hair spilled out around her like a fiery cloud. She was breathtakingly beautiful, and she was his. The universe had gifted him with everything he ever wanted. Now, all he had to do to hang onto it was keep her safe, find a murderer and his cohorts, and take down an entire pharma cartel.

He chuckled and planted a slow, lingering kiss on her sweet lips. "I'm starting to think things were easier back when I was a soldier. The only person I had to worry about was Dash, and the only responsibility we had was to get the information and get out alive."

"Now, you're responsible for the safety of the entire station, not to mention much of the Drift, you've got a bunch of bloodthirsty pharma dealers trying to kill you, and your girlfriend is dabbling in corporate espionage. Things probably were easier before, but there's one thing that you'd be missing."

"What's that?" he asked as he managed to roll over without falling off the bed. Now she was on top of him, and he was lying on his back with his feet hanging over the edge of her bed.

"Me. Back then, there was no way we could have been together. Now, no matter how hard things get, at least we have each other. I'd sacrifice a great many things if it meant keeping you and Dash."

He stroked her hair back from her face and marveled at the woman in his arms. There was a core of steel inside of her, and it made her all the more amazing to him. "You're going to be stuck with us both for a very long time. We thought we lost you once already. No matter how much we screw up from here on in, you have to know that we're not letting you go. You're all we've been dreaming of for years."

She surprised him by starting to hum the song he had sung for her on their first date, and then she melted his heart when she sang one of the lines in an achingly perfect alto. *"I have everything I dreamed of in the palm of my hand..."*

"You can sing?" He was already thinking of ways to get her up on stage with him.

"A little." She said, dismissing her talent with a shrug. "When I was a kid I discovered that busking in the shopping hubs and transit tunnels paid better than stealing. I sang, one of my younger brothers could make a drum out of anything you can imagine, and another managed to acquire a battered, old guitar. We weren't starving, exactly, but our family didn't have money for anything but the necessities. Too many mouths to feed, especially when we were all kids."

"You sing more than a little. If you ever quit your job at Astek, I suspect T'arv would happily hire you for gigs at the club."

Some of the light faded from her eyes at his mention of Astek. "What is it?" he asked.

"I quit my job. I can't work for any corporation involved in the Resource Wars. Not now that I know what they did—what they all agreed to do to Cynder and the others."

"It's probably time you told me what's on that data stick. Is it even safe to have it here? Won't they find out you've got hold of something you shouldn't have?

"I'll tell you what I uncovered, and who helped me, as soon as you tell me more about Len. How did Dash recover his memories? Where is he right now? Why would Len turn traitor?"

Mack pressed a finger to her lips and winked. "If you give me a moment, I'll check in with Dash."

"Tell him I said hi."

Mack opened the internal comm channel between himself and Dash. *"Got time for a quick sitrep?"*

"I'm not talking to you right now. It's been an age since the link between us has worked in reverse, but I've been dealing with a non-stop barrage of sex feedback for the last ten minutes. Do you have any idea how hard it is to run a manhunt like that?"

"Why didn't you say something? I didn't even know I was projecting. I can't control it the way you can."

"I know, and I'm not such a jerk I was going to interrupt your moment. I take it we've been forgiven for our stupidity?"

"We have. You anywhere with finding that asshole and whoever is working with him?"

Dash's frustration bled through their link. *"Nothing. We've got him on security vids leaving the Nova Club not long after Lieksa. He followed her for a while, but then broke off. Probably when he saw that Lieksa wasn't alone. We tracked him to a bank of mag-lifts, and then he vanishes like a* fraxxing *phantom."*

"You thinking what I'm thinking?"

"He's going to make a play for Lieksa. It's the only move he has left. She told him she might be able to restore my memories, and that makes her his prime target. If he can't get to her tonight, I bet he'll make a run for it."

"Keep looking. Lieksa and I are secure where we are."

Lieksa tapped his chest to get his attention. "Is he okay?"

"He's okay. He'd rather be here with us right now, but otherwise, he's fine."

"Tell him to catch the lying son of a starbeast quickly, then he can join us. Though I really don't think the three of us would fit on this bed."

"He said he'll do his best to finish this up quickly."

"You should be with him instead of here, with me," she said.

"No, I shouldn't be. One of us needs to be here with you. You told Len you could restore Dash's digital memories. The only way he gets away with what he's done is if Dash never remembers. That makes you his number one target. You, and whoever he's got working with him. Someone killed Crews while Len was still recovering, which means he's got at least one partner out there."

She closed her eyes and sighed. "I'm sorry I didn't listen to you before. You were right. I was in danger. But, if we let everyone know Dash has his memory back, wouldn't that knock me off the list of targets?"

"You were in danger, yes, but we could have handled it better." He wrapped a strand of her hair around his finger and tugged at it until she opened her eyes again. "I don't believe you're going to be safe until we have Len in custody. Even if Dash doesn't need you to fix his memories anymore, you'd still to be a target. You're important to us and Len knows it. The fastest way to get to us is to hurt you."

She nodded. "So I need to stay out of the way and let you do your job. I understand. I don't like feeling useless, though."

He smiled at her. "You're not useless. Don't forget, we know Len's the traitor because of you. If we hadn't seen him talking to you, Dash's memory wouldn't have been jarred. It was that gesture Len made that triggered everything."

"I like that version of events. I'm going with that as my official story." She reached out and pointed to the data stick on the shelf beside them. "You asked me if it was safe to have that here. While I was waiting for you, I made several copies, encrypted them, and sent them to others. Even if they find that one, they'll never find them all. The truth is going to come out one way or another."

"And what about you? What if they find out you were behind the information getting out?"

"I was careful. The tech I used is top of the line, almost impossible to detect. Even if they do find out they were breached, they won't know how, or who orchestrated it. Only one person knows what I did, and he escorted me out of the building tonight and made sure I got home safely. Zale isn't going to say anything. As it turns out, he already knew the truth, but he couldn't tell anyone. I think he's relieved to know someone is going to do something about it."

"Zale knows?"

Lieksa filled him in on what had happened, and by the time she was done his mind was busy sorting through all this new information. Things were more complicated now, but that didn't matter. All that really mattered was keeping Lieksa safe.

CHAPTER FIFTEEN

Lieksa slept fitfully, but she wouldn't have slept at all if Mack wasn't with her. Having him back in her life made everything feel right, even if it really wasn't. Dash was out hunting a traitor they'd all trusted, the corporations were keeping life-ruining secrets, and it felt as if the number of people she trusted could be counted on one hand. Yet, crammed in beside Mack on her tiny bed, his arms around her and his chest rising and falling with every slow breath he took, she had faith that everything was going to work out somehow, for all of them. Well, everyone but Len. As far as she was concerned, he deserved to be thrown out the nearest airlock or tossed into the heart of a star.

"You need to sleep," Mack said, his voice a soft rumble by her ear.

"So do you."

"I'm a cyborg, remember? I can go for days without sleep if I have to. My medi-bots will keep me on my feet for as long as I need to be. You have no such advantage, so try to rest. If I hear anything from Dash, you'll be the first to know."

"It must be strange not to need sleep. What do you think about in the middle of the night and there's nothing to do?"

"I'd think about you. On the hospital ship, you were my distraction. Afterward, you were my fantasy, and now, you're reality."

She smiled and snuggled in closer to his side. "I think Dash has competition for being the charming one in this relationship. All these years, I dreamed about the two of you, too. No matter how this ends, I'm glad we got a chance to be together."

"This isn't going to end, Lieksa. Not in this lifetime, and not in the one that comes after."

"Everything ends—" she started to say, but her argument was cut short by a muffled chiming from her comm device.

The device was still in her pants pocket, and her pants were still in the pile of clothing they'd created in their earlier rush to get naked. She had to climb over Mack's naked body to retrieve it, which created the opportunity for all sorts of distractions along the way.

When she finally dug out her comms and answered it, she was out of breath and sprawled in an ungainly tangle on the floor. In her rush, she didn't check to see who was calling. "Hello?"

"Lieksa, it's Len. Len Daniels. I'm so glad you answered. You need to get here. Mack's been wounded, and it's not looking good. Are you at home? I'll come get you myself."

Icy tendrils wove down her spine, weaving a pattern of fear and loathing as they went. She didn't have to fake the quaver in her voice as she asked the questions he would be expecting. "Mack's hurt? How? Where? I'm home. Please hurry. I want to see Mack right away."

"I'll be there soon. Dash would have called you himself, but he's with Mack right now. I'll tell you all about it once we're on the way there, okay? I'm two minutes out. Don't open the door or talk to anyone. It's not safe."

"Okay."

She disconnected the call and blew out a breath before looking up at Mack. He was out of bed and pulling on his clothes as fast as he could, but his eyes never left her as she caught him up on the conversation, keeping her voice low, just in case. "That bastard said you were injured and Dash was sending him to fetch me before it was too late. He'll be here in two minutes. He didn't even ask me where I lived. He already knew! *Veth*, if you weren't here, safe and sound, I'd have believed him. How the hell did he find me?"

Mack helped her to her feet and handed her several pieces of clothing, then pulled her into his arms and crushed his lips to hers. "You were brilliant. As for how he found you, he could have simply looked you up. He might've slipped a tracker on you when he saw you tonight, though.

Did he touch you at all?" he asked once he released her again.

She was going to say no, then remembered the odd way Len had touched her shoulder before leaving the table. "He might have. I'll check my clothes later to be sure. What happens when he gets here?" she asked as she dressed.

"I've already let Dash know we're about to have company. He and the task force are on the way, but they're not going to get here before Len does. When he arrives, we've got two choices."

She cocked her head, her fingers frozen on the fastenings of her pants. "You're giving me a choice?"

The look he shot her was full of frustration and worry, but he nodded. "I am. You don't respond well to orders, so I'm trying something new."

"What are the options?"

"Option one: you go to the bathroom and stay there until I tell you it's safe to come out and I take on Len when he gets here."

"I don't like that option. What if he's not alone?"

"That leaves option two: you answer the door, but stay off to one side so no one can take a shot at you. Tell him you need to grab your repair kit or something. Then try to get him to follow you inside. I'll be waiting out of sight, and the moment he's through the door, you hide in the bathroom while I deal with the threat."

She frowned at him. "I see some overlap in these plans, but since I'm not the one genetically bred and cybernetically enhanced to be a soldier, I'm not going to argue. Option two it is. See? That wasn't so bad, was it?"

He scowled at her. "Now is not the time for sass. This would be a lot simpler if I could just kill the bastard, but we need him alive. A fight in tight quarters like this…there are a lot of variables. Once that door is open, you head straight for the bathroom and out of the line of fire. I can deal with anything but losing you."

She nodded, then finished getting dressed, leaving her shoes off because it seemed like an obvious reason for her to need another minute to get ready. Her heart was pounding, and her hands were shaking the whole time, but she was determined to see this through. The bastard coming for her had tried to kill everyone she cared about, and he had to be stopped.

When the door chime sounded, she nearly jumped out of her skin. Mack placed a steadying hand on her shoulder, and she leaned into him for a brief second while she pulled herself together. *I can do this.*

"Len, is that you?" she asked through the intercom.

"It's me. We need to hurry. Open the door."

Mack had dimmed the lights so that most of her cubby was dark, making it easier for him to stay out of sight. He was pressed against the wall on the other side of the door, one hand already on the access panel. He nodded once, and she moved to one side as he punched in the code to override his security measures and open the door.

"You ready?" Len demanded before the door was even fully open.

"Almost. Still need my shoes. Have you heard anything else? How's Mack? What happened?" She kept hitting him with questions in an attempt to keep his focus on her.

"Same thing that happened to Crews, I guess. Someone tried to take him out."

He stepped inside and she deliberately moved backward, her face buried in her hands as she sobbed loudly. "I can't believe this is happening. It's so awful!"

He followed her exactly as she hoped he would, putting him in the middle of the room with Mack behind him. The door shut, and all hell broke loose.

She dropped her hands in time to see Mack charge toward Len and she scrambled to get out of the way. The plan to get to the bathroom had seemed practical enough in theory, but the reality was that having two huge men battling it out in her small residence meant there was no clear path for her to take. They were grappling and punching, and while it was clear Mack was winning, Len was a tough, well-trained officer, and he was fighting like a man with nothing left to lose.

She dodged around them as best she could, but her best wasn't enough to keep her out of harm's way. Len's out-flung fist struck her face as she tried to slip past, and she yelped in surprise and pain. Starbursts of light exploded and danced in front of her eyes, making it impossible for her to see.

"Lieksa!" Mack called her name frantically.

She tried to get out of the way, but before she could take more than a single, unsteady step, a hand clamped around her wrist and jerked her back.

"Where do you think you're going?" Len demanded. He twisted her captured arm behind her back with enough force to make her want to cry out again, but she bit her lip and refused to utter a sound. She wasn't going to give him the satisfaction of knowing she was in pain. Something cold and sharp pressed to her throat hard enough that if she moved more than a fraction of an inch, it was going to cut her.

"If you hurt her, they'll never find all the pieces of your body, Daniels."

The man she loved was standing only a few feet away, but she barely recognized him right now. His voice was as cold as the vacuum of space, and his hazel eyes were dark with fury. His hands were curled into fists at his sides, and as the last stars cleared her vision, she noticed there were traces of blood on his knuckles and a nasty cut on his cheek.

Len snarled in frustration, the knife he held digging into her flesh. "If you so much as twitch, I'll do more than hurt her. I'll slice her throat and let you watch as she bleeds to death. I didn't want it to go this way. Only you and Dash were supposed to die. With you gone, I'd take over as head of the taskforce, the cartel would pay off my debts, and everyone would have been happy. I'd be in charge, instead of taking orders from a couple of freaks, and the cartel could run their business in peace. Simple *fraxxing* arrangement. Then Dash doesn't die like he's supposed to, Crews figures out I'm the one who dosed him so he was too sick to work the day of the raid, and it all starts coming apart at the seams."

"Let me go, Len. You said you didn't want to hurt me. You don't have to. Let me go, and this can end with everyone still breathing." Lieksa forced herself to relax as much as she could.

"Not going to happen. You're my ticket out of here. I'm a wanted man, now. My only chance is to get the hell away from the Drift, and they're not going to let that happen unless I bring insurance. Isn't that right, Mack?"

"You think taking a hostage is going to improve the situation? It's not. You don't even have a ship, Daniels. There's nowhere for you to go. The best thing you can do for yourself is to let Lieksa go and surrender."

"Like I told your girlfriend not fifteen seconds ago, that's not going to happen. You're not in charge here, Mack. You should never have been in charge. It should have been me!"

Len's voice cracked with emotion, and his grip on Lieksa loosened a little. It was the opening she had been waiting for. Without warning, she grabbed at the knife blade and went limp, dropping through his arms toward the floor. The knife sliced deep into her fingers, but she ignored the pain. When she'd dropped far enough that her knees were bent, she tensed and then straightened up as fast as she could. The back of her head slammed into Len's chin and nose, and once again starbursts danced in her vision.

After that, everything seemed to happen at once. Len screeched and released her to clutch his battered face. Mack was on him instantly, tearing into him with a violence she could hear, but not see.

Lieksa managed to stagger a few paces, but she tripped and went down hard, cracking her forehead on the edge of her bed on the way to the floor. The starbursts of light faded away, but her vision didn't return. Instead, everything was veiled in a gray haze. Her hand throbbed with pain that only worsened when she made a fist with it to try to slow the bleeding.

She caught flashes of the fight between Mack and Len, but it was like watching a video with a faulty feed. The focus was off, and the images flickered and jumped. It wasn't more than a few seconds before there was a reverberating thud, and then the sounds of fighting stopped.

"Lieksa? Angel, please open your eyes. Talk to me."

Until Mack pointed it out, she hadn't realized her eyes were closed. Something told her that probably wasn't a good thing. She forced her eyes open and lifted her head to see him staring at her with a worried expression. "I should have gone with option one, huh?"

"Based on the amount of bleeding you're doing, I'd have to agree. Dash is going to come through that door any second, and he's going to want to know how you are. What should I tell him?" He tenderly stroked back a strand of hair from her face.

"Tell him I broke that bastard's nose, and I probably have a concussion. And a bit of a cut on the neck." She held up her bloody fist and tried to muster a smile, but her head was full of grinding pain and too many parts of her hurt to make it work. "I think I'm going to need a few stitches in my hand, too. I envy you those medi-bots right now. You'll be healed up before I make it to medical."

"He's going to kill me for letting you get hurt," Mack murmured as he gathered her into his arms as gently as he could and cradled her in his lap, one hand pressed to the bloodied lump on her forehead.

"Tell him I wanted option two. My choice. I'm sorry you got hurt, though. My fault. I didn't get to the bathroom fast enough." Her eyes fluttered closed again as a wave of nauseating vertigo overtook her.

Somewhere in the distance a door opened, and she could hear voices asking questions in urgent tones, but it was all happening too far away for her to pay much attention. The pain was fading too, and she was happy to let everything drift away. It had been a hell of a night, and she was ready to sleep.

* * * *

Dash came through the door to Lieksa's home with a team of men at his back, all of them intent on bringing the traitor who had killed one of their own to justice. He wasn't prepared to see the woman he loved lying battered, bleeding, and unconscious in Mack's arms. The rest of his team poured in and secured Len, who was face down in a pool of what Dash hoped was his own blood.

"Dammit, Mack. Keep her safe. Wasn't that the deal? How badly is she hurt?" he demanded as he crouched by Mack to take a better look at Lieksa.

"I tried to keep her out of it. She had her own ideas. She wanted me to tell you this was her choice, and that she was the one who busted Len's nose. She's very proud of that. She's got a concussion, a wound on her neck, and a nasty slash on her hand where she held onto his knife blade. Nothing the doc can't fix up, though."

He glanced up at Mack, surprised. "She decked him? Our angel? And what do you mean, she grabbed his knife?"

"She head-butted him, actually. I think we're missing some key background information on our girl. She mentioned tonight that she grew up in a hive city back on Earth, and I watched her take down Len with a move that was straight streetfighter. She's tougher than I ever gave her credit for. Braver, too. Medical is already on their way here. Once they arrive, I'll tell you all about it. I'll even show you. I may not be able to record every detail like you can, but you'll be able to see what happened."

Len groaned as Dirk and Lance hauled him to his feet and started to lug him out of the room.

"I don't suppose his partner was standing out there with his hands up, ready to surrender and make this easy for us?" Mack asked.

"No such luck. We've got Daniels, though. I don't think Len's the kind to endure interrogation for long. More likely he'll confess quickly in hopes of getting a deal."

Dash looked around at the bloodstained and upturned contents of Lieksa's home. "When this is all done, you and I need to talk about her living arrangements. This neighborhood clearly isn't safe."

Mack nodded. "We need to talk about a few things, including what Lieksa discovered about the corporations. I'll catch you up on the way to medical." He blew out a tired breath. "It's been a busy night."

Dash reached out to take Lieksa's uninjured hand in his. He needed to be connected to her. To feel her even if she didn't know he was there. "It has, but we're all still here. I'm chalking this up as a win."

"Me, too. With what's coming our way, we're going to need to enjoy our victories while we can."

Dash didn't know exactly what Mack meant, but that didn't matter. Whatever was coming, they'd face it together.

CHAPTER SIXTEEN

Dash kept his arm around Lieksa's shoulders as they made the walk from medical to the Nova Club. It wasn't a long way, but considering she had only been released from the med center half an hour ago, he wasn't taking any chances. Dr. Jefferies might think that two days was enough recovery time, but he wasn't convinced. Judging by how close Mack was sticking while they made their way through the mid-day crowd, he wasn't convinced, either.

Len was being interrogated somewhere far from the Drift, but he wasn't the only threat they were facing. The Drojo Cartel was scattered and on the run. Even with the information Len was providing, hunting them all down would be a long, dangerous process. The killer working with Len turned out to be an assassin for hire who was only known as Reaper. Apart from a long list of kills stretching back several years, there was no other data. No ID, no known associates, nothing. Whoever he was, he was still out there.

"I'm fine, you know," Lieksa said giving him a gentle shoulder bump that pulled him back to the present.

"I know. But the last time I let you out of my sight you ended up with a concussion, sliced tendons in your hand, and a slashed throat. With that in mind, you can expect me to be feeling overprotective for the foreseeable future."

She laughed and shook her head. "I finally convince Mack to stop treating me like a Tiskalian ice orchid, and now you're doing it. I can't win, can I?"

He lowered his head to whisper in her ear. "There is no way in hell either one of us are going to stop trying to protect you, ever. Most especially not when we're all about to be neck-deep in this conspiracy you've uncovered."

"I only wanted to help Cynder and the others. I had no idea how deep this gravity well went," she whispered back.

"Even if you had known, you would've gone ahead, anyway. It was the right thing to do. One thing I've learned is that you always do the right thing, no matter what the cost."

"Yeah, but usually the risk is mine. This time, there's so much more at stake."

He could see she wanted to say more, but this wasn't the place or time. From now on, they were going to take every precaution in order to protect themselves, starting with this meeting. As far as anyone else knew, it was a private party to celebrate Len's capture and Lieksa's release from medical. To the handful of people attending, it was anything but a celebration. They were coming together to share information and start making plans.

Zura met them at the door of the club, greeting the three of them with a bright smile and a hug. *Why were all the women they knew huggers? Well, all but Cynder.*

"It's good to see you up and around, Lieksa. How's the hand? Come on in. Everyone else is already here."

Lieksa held out her newly healed hand, palm up, to show the faint pink line that crossed her fingers. "The hand is fine. Alyson wants me to take it easy for a few days to give everything time to finish healing, but she says it won't even scar. The healing accelerants worked perfectly."

The club was relatively quiet for now, with only a few hardcore players at the tables and a dozen or so patrons enjoying the bar's other amenities. No one so much as glanced up from their drinks as they passed through. Most of the club was shrouded in its usual shadow, but the area around the bar was lit up with dozens of holographic candles in a variety of shapes, sizes, and colors. The Festival of Light wasn't until tomorrow evening, but it seemed Nova was already decorated.

Zura led them to one of the staff-only entrances and opened it by pressing her hand to a scanner set into the wall beside the door. In the last few days, the Armas family had made some upgrades to their club's security.

Lieksa followed Zura through the door and into the quiet service corridor beyond. It was strange how disconnected this part of the club felt from the space they had just left. There was no heavy bass music here, and the color scheme was so ordinary she might have been walking through Astek Corp headquarters instead of one of the most notorious clubs on the Drift.

It was a brief walk to yet another door, and then Zura was gesturing for her to enter and join the rest of the group. They were waiting for them in one of the larger private party rooms, and despite the solemn reasons they were all there, the atmosphere was light, and they were greeted with smiles. A large, battered table took up most of the space, with enough chairs set around it to accommodate everyone. There was a food dispenser installed along one wall and a small, multi-purpose bar that looked like a miniature version of the one that ran the length of the Nova Club outside.

From the second she walked into the room, Lieksa found herself the center of attention. Everyone wanted to wish her well and to thank her for what she'd done. She hadn't been expecting it, and soon she was blushing as she kept trying to insist she hadn't done anything special. Eventually, she excused herself and let Dash and Mack escort her to a chair at one end of the table. Once she was seated, they claimed the seats on either side of her.

"There are more of us than I realized," Lieksa murmured as she looked around the room.

"And they're all here to do their part to make things right, just like you did," Dash replied.

There were over a dozen people present. It was comforting to know that whatever happened next, none of them would be facing it alone. Kit and Luke Armas were present of course, along with their wife, Zura and their batch sister, Cynder. Cynder's cyborg husbands, Toro and Jaeger were talking with Lance, Dirk, and Blade at one end of the table, while Alyson was chatting to a good looking, dark haired man that Mack told her was Zura's half-brother, Royan.

Zale and another Torski male were standing in one corner. The other male had to be Denz, Zale's cousin. Supposedly they had more information to share, which was a brave move, considering they both still worked for Astek. She had tried to talk Zale out of being involved any more than he already was, but he wouldn't be deterred. He said he was done keeping the corporations' secrets.

Eventually, everyone took their seats, and Alyson rose to her feet. "Is everything ready?" she asked, looking at Kit.

"No one outside this room will be able to hear or see anything we do. It's as secure as we could make it," the club's head of security replied.

"Alright then." Alyson squared her shoulders and looked around the table at everyone. "As you all know, two days ago Lieksa retrieved a treasure trove of data from Astek's servers. I now know what was done to Cynder and the other cyborg women. More importantly, the data included an antidote, and I'm working on synthesizing it. It's going to take me a little time to get all the ingredients together since we don't want the corporations having any inkling of what I'm trying to do. They're already concerned enough about what I'm up to that they sent a couple of lawyers to speak with me. They've backed off, for now, because I told them that I didn't have anything to do with repairing Dash's implants. That was all handled by Lieksa, who was an Astek employee at the time."

"But you can make it work? You're sure? They can't stop you, can they?" Cynder asked, leaning forward in her chair.

"Now that I know what I'm dealing with, yes, I'm sure I can reverse it. And no, I'm not going to let them stop me. That's why it's so important that what we're doing stay a secret." Alyson smiled at Cynder. "For now, you're the only one of the affected women who will know. I hate keeping good news a secret, but in this case, we have to. No one outside this room can know what we're doing. There's too much at stake."

Alyson paused and placed her hand on the data tablet lying on the table beside her. "There's more at stake than any of us knew."

Lieksa knew what the doctor was about to say, but that didn't make it any easier to hear. She squeezed Mack and Dash's hands as Alyson activated a holo-projection that filled the air above the table.

Alyson pointed to the projection. "Over the last two days, I've read through as much of the data as I could. My main focus was to find out what was done and how to reverse it, but while I was reading, I noticed something else. It's a phrase that popped out at me, and once I started looking for it, I found it repeated several times throughout the data. When referring to the substance that rendered the cyborg females infertile, they always state it was given to every *released* female."

There were several horrified gasps and muttered curses as the meaning of that phrase sank in. If it was only given to the ones who were released, where were the others? Who were they, and why hadn't they been granted their freedom with the rest?

"I helped the doctor review everything, at least, as much as she'd let me between the tests and constantly insisting I get more rest," Lieksa said, and there were chuckles from around the table.

"Once Alyson noticed the pattern, I determined something else of interest. None of the documents that use that phrase are from Astek Corp. We can't tell whose they are, because the names were redacted. It looks like I might have stumbled on a cache of information Astek stole or acquired from somewhere else."

Zale spoke up, his normally booming voice subdued and quiet. "I was part of the taskforce who created the substance the corporations used. There was no mention of anyone not being released. If I'd have known, I wouldn't have kept my silence for so long."

Cynder had already been told about Zale's involvement. She said she had come to terms with it, but there was still a moment of unease as everyone waited for her reaction. Cynder's temper was somewhat legendary on the station, and so was her streak of victories in the fighting cage. If she was still holding a grudge, it could get ugly, fast.

"You're here, helping to undo what was done." Cynder glanced over at Lieksa and smiled. "I've come to understand that cyborgs weren't the only ones lied to and used during the wars. What matters is that we've all come together to make this right. However we can, whatever it takes."

"Thank you, Cynder." Zale rose to his feet. "You all know who I am, and who I work for. I'm here today because I've decided it's time to take a stand. You're going to need someone on the inside to help you obtain some of the information you need. Denz and I are willing to do that."

"That will make things easier for us, but it's a hell of a risk for the two of you. It's appreciated," Kit said.

"There's something else I came here to talk about. I know why Zura survived the medi-bot transfusion she received from her husbands," Zale said.

"What? How?" Zura asked, her silver eyes wide with shock.

"Medi-bots are genetically keyed to their carriers. It's one of the reasons cyborgs were created in batches. It meant each batch shared enough of the same DNA that we didn't have to adjust the nanotech for every individual. This technology will not activate if the host body doesn't have the right genetic markers."

"But she's not related to us," Luke insisted.

"Directly related? No. That's highly unlikely given cyborgs were designed in a lab from the chromosomes up, but the DNA you were built with came from someone, and apparently you and your wife share a common ancestor. There's no other explanation."

"You're sure? We're not even Astek cyborg designs," Kit said.

"I'm positive. I was on the team that first designed the medi-bots all cyborgs carry. Every corporation reverse-engineered them from our designs. That happened a lot, which is why cyborgs are so similar despite being built by warring factions."

"My relative's DNA was used? I never knew that. I wonder whose it was. I suppose that wouldn't be hard to find out. Doc, can we test for that?"

"We can, and I think we should," Alyson agreed.

"No one knew the source of the original genetic material. At least, no one at my pay grade."

Zura blushed, her blue skin changing shades and her natural striations darkening to tiger-like stripes across her face and neck. "We should do the testing soon, Alyson." She placed a hand on her stomach and beamed at everyone. "I'm pregnant. With twins of all things. We're keeping it a secret for as long as we can. When the corporations find out, there's no telling what they'll do. This is what they're afraid of—the medi-bot technology passing into the general population. My babies will be born with the nanotech already part of them."

"No matter what happens, there's no way in hell we're letting anyone threaten you or those babies, sis. Isn't that right?" Royan asked, his voice carrying over the din.

Right!" The group responded.

There was a crush to congratulate Zura, so Lieksa hung back, happy to wait with Dash and Mack. They had taken turns staying with her since she got hurt, but there hadn't been any time for the three of them to be together. She was looking forward to spending some time alone with them both.

Zale pushed his way through the crowd and made his way to the small bar where Lieksa was standing.

"I'm glad to see you've recovered from your last adventure." He paused to pull something out of his pocket and set it on the bar beside her. "Ready for the next one?"

She looked at the object he'd set down and frowned. It looked like a standard medical injector. "What is it?"

"A gift for you. I didn't turn over all my research and equipment when I left my old job. There are enough medi-bots in this injector to create a permanent colony in your bloodstream if you decide to use it."

"You kept some?" She didn't know what surprised her more; the fact her normally by-the-book former boss had kept forbidden technology or the fact he was giving it to her.

"You think you've got a monopoly on holding onto illegal tech?" he asked. "Like a certain data-mining widget that seems to be missing from your old workshop."

She ignored the subtle barb and stared at the injector. Inside that device was the solution to one of her greatest fears: that she would grow old and die long before Mack or Dash did. "I thought you said they had to be genetically keyed to the DNA of their host body?"

"I've made some improvements on the original design. These medi-bots don't require a genetic key."

"Holy *fraxx*. You didn't settle for stealing them, you tweaked them, too."

"This is my life's work. I couldn't let them destroy the greatest thing I ever helped create. The loss would be too much. One day, I hope they can be used to help all our races live longer, healthier lives. This tech has so much potential for good, maybe it can outweigh some of the mistakes I've made."

She picked up the injector and cradled it in her hand. "So, if I used these, I'd live as long as Mack and Dash?"

"You'd heal like they do. You'd be resistant to disease, too. I can't be sure you'd have the same lifespan because no one knows how long the cyborgs will live, but I'm confident it would be close."

"What are the risks?" Mack asked.

"There aren't any. Well, not from the medi-bots. If anyone finds out, Lieksa would be a target in the same way Zura is, but I think we're all going to be targeted from here on in. Doing the right thing is going to come with a fair bit of risk for all of us."

"Why does it matter to you how long you'll live?" Dash asked.

"I love you both, but I can't help thinking about what our future would be like. I'll get old and frail, and you'll both still be young and healthy. How could that possibly work?"

Both men glowered at her with almost identical stormy expressions. "It'll work because we love you. That's how," Mack retorted.

Zale chuckled and took a step back. "I'll take that as my cue to leave you three to discuss the details. It's not an easy decision. If you decide not to, you can return the injector to me. I'll be making the same offer to everyone else here, eventually, but I wanted you to be the first."

"If I decide to do this, what do I have to do?" she asked.

"Inject yourself with the contents of that vial. That's it. The nanotech will start to replicate immediately. Once it's done, you won't be able to remove them, so be sure," Zale said.

"Thank you."

"You're welcome. I figured if we're all about to put our asses on the line, we might as well make sure we heal fast."

"Good thinking. You did this? Injected yourself?" she asked.

"Last night. Never saw the need until now, but once Denz and I decided to join your group, I did it, and so did he. I used to believe that one day the corporations would re-think their stance and allow everyone access to this technology. Now, I realize that's never going to happen. If we want things to change, we're going to have to *make* it happen."

Zale left, and she turned to Mack and Dash.

"Ready to go home?" Dash asked.

"Then we'll talk about Zale's gift, and what you want to do with it," Mack added.

"I'm almost ready. We need to talk to Zura and congratulate them, first. She is going to make the sweetest mother, and I bet those babies are going to be gorgeous."

"They're also going to be the most protected children in the galaxy. They've got an entire room full of people ready to defend them, and they're not even born yet," Mack said.

They made their way across the room to hand out hugs, backslaps, and congratulations. They said their goodbyes and promised to be back the next night to celebrate the Festival of Light with everyone.

She hadn't celebrated that holiday in years. Not since she had left Earth and her family. She told herself that celebrating the longest night of the year on a planet she no longer lived was a waste of time, but that wasn't the real reason. The holiday was all about spending time with friends and family. Everyone came together, eating and drinking and rejoicing in the reminder that no matter how dark it got, the light would always return again. It was a nice sentiment, but one she hadn't believed in for years. Not when her life seemed destined to remain in shadow. This year, everything was different, and she looked forward to celebrating the return of the light with the people who had become her new family.

CHAPTER SEVENTEEN

Dash was on edge. It wasn't a feeling he was overly familiar with, and he wasn't enjoying it. He wanted everything to go perfectly tonight, and their recent track record was a few light-years away from anything even resembling perfection.

"Did you to think I wouldn't notice that this isn't the way to my place?" Lieksa asked as they headed for the nearest bank of mag-lifts.

"You said you wanted to go home," Mack said.

"Home, as in my home, not yours. I thought I might pack a few things and then we could go to your place, that way I wouldn't have to go home again for a few days. I know you two still probably have to work, but I'm currently between jobs, so…"

"We'd love you to stay with us. In fact, we might have already been by your place to pick up a few things. You don't need to go home, angel. Everything you need is already waiting for you at our place."

She stopped walking, forcing them to stop, too, or leave her behind in the crowd. "You packed for me?"

"Well, yeah. You asked us to bring you some clothes and things so you could go to the party straight from medical. We decided to uh, keep going."

Her brows shot up. "How far did you go, exactly?"

"Do you really need to ask?" Mack asked.

"You packed it all." It wasn't a question.

Dash couldn't stop the wry chuckle that left his lips. "This isn't exactly the way we planned it, but after the last few weeks, that's not much of a surprise. Yes, we packed it all. We don't want you to come stay with us for a couple of days. We want you to live with us."

"Live with you. In your spacious, two-level home. Is this so you can protect me better?"

"It's actually a three-level home. You haven't seen the lower floor yet. As for protecting you, yes, that's part of the plan, but it's not the big reason." Mack said.

"And what's the big reason?" she asked, a lilt of laughter in her voice.

"We love you, and we want to share our life with you," Dash said, tugging her into his arms.

"You know, Mack's told me he loves me, but I'm pretty sure you haven't actually said anything about *your* feelings yet."

"You want a confession, sweetheart?" He lifted her into his arms and started to spin her around, making everyone stop and stare as he made his declaration. "I love you. From the ends of your gorgeous red hair to the tips of your toes. You're the center of my universe, and there is nothing in the cosmos that is ever going to change that. When we celebrate the Festival of Light tomorrow, the light I'm going to be thinking of, is you. So, what do you say, will you move in with us?"

She beamed at him. "I love you, too. I'm crazy in love with you both, and I've never been happier. Yes, I'll live with you. I really don't have much choice; you already moved all my stuff!"

Cheers and wolf whistles broke out all around them, and the angel in his arms blushed until her cheeks were a match for her hair.

"You can put me down now," she murmured.

"I could. Not going to, though." He shifted his grip so that she was cradled in his arms and started walking through the still cheering crowd.

"Show-off," Mack muttered as he fell in beside them.

"This, from the guy who sings on stage for fun," Dash shot back.

Lieksa reached out to Mack, who took her hand and held it as the three of them continued the walk home. All the knowing smiles and stares they garnered along the way kept her cheeks flushed the whole way home, but she didn't ask to be put down again until they were inside.

"Not just yet. There's something we want to show you," he told her. It was time for the second surprise.

Lieksa was too happy to protest over the fact she was still being carried around. She was starting to adjust to the reality that her men were always going to be like this, and it wasn't because they thought she was incapable of taking care of herself.

Mack walked to the far side of the entranceway and ran his hand over a door panel she had never noticed before. He vanished through the door as soon as it slid open, and Dash followed a few seconds later.

Curiosity ate at her as they descended a short flight of stairs and arrived in a non-descript room that looked more like an office than living space. There were two desks, a conference table with overhead digital display components, and a few scattered chairs. The walls were full of notes, diagrams, and pictures, but she was too far away to make out what any of it meant.

"You have an office at home, too? You two really need more hobbies," she said.

"This didn't happen until our real office got blown up. It was going to be temporary, but now I think we'll keep it. We can bring down another desk and make this a place for the three of us to track everything we find out about what the corporations are up to, and where the missing women might be," Dash explained.

"I think that's a great idea." She wanted to do a victory dance but settled for a happy bounce in Dash's arms. If they wanted her to work with them down here, that meant they weren't planning on keeping her distanced from whatever came next.

"Something else you should know. This level has hardened walls and can be made airtight. I have no idea why, or what used to be here back before Astek bought and reconfigured it, but if anything ever goes sideways, you get your ass down here and activate the security system. The console is over there. We'll scan your palm print and voice commands later," Mack pointed back toward the staircase and the console installed into the wall next to it.

"You can't help yourself, can you? You had to slip a bossy order in there."

Mack chuckled. "Like I told you before, that's never going to change. Besides, I distinctly remember you saying you should have gone with option one the last time I gave you a choice. Consider this space as an upgrade on hiding in your bathroom."

She looked around at the minimalist décor and laughed. "Speaking of which, does this place have a bathroom? If there's a chance we're going to be locked in here, that's going to be important."

"First door on your left," Dash said.

"The door on the right is a pantry and storeroom, and there's a basic food dispenser in there as well. We figured if we were going to be working down here, we were going to need coffee and food," Mack said.

"And the second door on the left is what? A spa? Your own private swimming pool?" she asked, once again amazed by how large their home was.

"It can be both. Sort of. I think it's easier to show you than explain." Dash lifted her higher into his arms and brushed a quick kiss to her lips before carrying her over to the last door.

"Computer, activate program Lieksa's Homecoming One," Mack said.

"Program now running."

Lieksa sat up in Dash's arms and turned to stare at them both in disbelief. "You have a sim pod? Here? Holy *fraxx*, those cost a fortune!" The interactive hologram technology was popular on long-haul freighters and mining ships that would spend months at a time away from civilization. They could be rented by the hour at specialty shops all over the Drift, but she had never heard of anyone privately owning one.

"Some things are worth the scrip," was all Dash said.

The door opened and revealed an impossible wonderland on the other side. Snow fell in fat, white flakes that drifted out of a slate gray sky and everything was covered with a thick, fluffy blanket of snow. It looked like she was standing at the edge of a forest clearing, and directly across from her was a tiny cabin with smoke rising from the chimney and icicles hanging from the eaves. She was so taken with the scenery, it took some time before it occurred to her that what she was seeing couldn't possibly fit inside a standard pod. This was much, much larger.

"How?" she blurted, pointing into the room.

"Scrip. Spend enough of it, and you can have a sim room instead of a pod. Dash and I knew we were going to be out here for a long time, maybe the rest of our lives. Since we wouldn't be going planet-side again, we decided to bring the planets to us."

"Incredible," she murmured as Dash carried her into the simulation. The cold was shocking, especially after living on the station where the temperature was constant.

"We picked this program for you. The doc mentioned you had never seen real snow, so we thought you might like to experience the next best thing," Dash said.

"I know we're a day early, but we thought we could celebrate the Festival of Light tonight. Just the three of us. We've got a lot to celebrate this year. More than I ever imagined possible. And we still need to talk about what Zale offered you."

She laughed and wiggled until Dash put her down. Her light clothing was no barrier to the ice and cold, but she didn't care. She wanted to play.

"I would love to spend the night here. I want to build a snowman, and make snow angels, and do all the things I've only read about." She tipped her head back so that the flakes fell on her face, melting the moment they made contact. "This is amazing. Thank you. Now I know this is here, I may never leave."

Mack wrapped a blanket around her shoulders and nuzzled his lips to her neck. "So you don't get cold."

She laughed and turned to kiss him before running into the clearing, kicking up snow in her wake. "Come on, let's try and build a snowman together. I bet you've never done that either!"

They quickly discovered that making snow sculptures was cold, wet, work. By the time they had one misshapen figure completed, she was shivering, and even her durable cyborg lovers were looking a little chilly.

They headed for the tiny cabin, tumbling through the door together in their rush to get into the welcoming warmth. It amazed her that the simulation could be so detailed. While they were outside, she had forgotten that none of it was real.

The cabin was cozy. There was a small kitchen off one end, and a fire burning in the large fireplace at the other. The rest of the space was taken up by a bed big enough for all three of them. By unspoken agreement, they all stripped out of their wet clothes and hung them on pegs on the wall nearest the fire.

"We should have brought a change of clothes." she said as she peeled off her dripping socks.

"Already taken care of. Clothes are under the bed, and there's a feast stashed in the kitchen courtesy of T'arv and Nadia." Dash sat on the edge of the bed and crooked his finger. "Come here, sweetheart, and bring that injector with you."

She stuck out her tongue and shook her head, sending droplets of water flying. "Say please, pushy man."

Mack chuckled, then scooped her into his arms, snagged the injector from its spot on the mantelpiece and carried her, squirming and laughing, over to the bed.

"Please," he deadpanned as he dropped her into the middle of the mattress, letting her fall far enough to bounce a bit on impact.

Still feeling playful, she stretched out, showing off every inch of her naked body before turning her head to look at Dash, then Mack. "So, I'm here. Now what?"

"Now we talk about this," Mack held up the injector.

"There's nothing to talk about. I want to use it. I don't want to grow old and die and miss out on time I could have had with you. We've lost enough time already."

Dash sighed. "It's going to mean you're a bigger target than you already are."

"Not if we keep it a secret. I'm certainly not going to go around advertising the fact I'm loaded with nanotech. That would put Zale at risk, too."

Mack knelt on the bed, head bowed as he looked at the injector in his hand. "Before you do this, I think you need to understand something."

"What?" she asked, bracing for some sort of lecture.

"For as long as you live, you're going to belong to us. It won't matter if that's an hour or a century. So be sure you want to be with Dash and me for the rest of your life because we're never letting you go."

Tears welled up in her eyes, making her vision blur as she reached out a hand to each of them. "I'm sure."

"I'm glad you came back to us, angel," Dash murmured and moved toward her, gathering her into his arms and kissing her.

"Me, too," Mack agreed, settling his big body behind her, one hand reaching around to cup her breast.

They had her trapped between them, stroking and kissing every part of her until she was half wild with need. She was so hot that if she stepped outside, she would probably melt a hole in the snow.

Mack moved her hair off her neck and leaned in to blaze a trail of butterfly kisses up the side of her throat. He was so close she could feel the thick length of his cock pressed against her back. Dash had her pulled halfway into his lap, his cock trapped against her thigh. He was toying with her breasts, his nimble fingers tugging and tweaking her nipples until every touch sent a jolt of pleasure sizzling straight to her clit. His hungry kisses kept her breathless, tongues entwined, mouths sealed together in a give and take that made her ache for more. She needed them inside of her, loving her, taking her to the heights of pleasure so they could soar together.

"I love you so much," Dash said, sliding his hand between her legs to cup her sex and tease her with the tips of his fingers.

"Tell us who has your heart. Who are you going to spend forever with?" Mack asked.

"You have my heart, Mack, and you, Dash. You're who I'm going to spend forever with. It was always supposed to be the two of you."

"You're our angel," Mack said.

She felt something cold press against her neck.

"You're sure about forever? Last chance to opt out, sweetheart."

She kissed Dash again, then tipped her head to one side, offering her throat to Mack and the injector she knew he held to her skin. "I'm sure."

A brief sting, a faint hiss, and it was done. Her whole life changed in a matter of seconds.

"Ours now." Mack nuzzled the spot where he'd injected her, soothing it with gentle kisses.

Dash grinned at her, his eyes gleaming with mischief. "I wonder how long it'll take for your new endurance to kick in. With what I have planned for you, you're going to need it."

"Very romantic," she retorted, then leaned back against Mack. "Is he always going to be like this?"

"I'm afraid so. You took us on as is. No refunds or exchanges," Dash said before slanting a hard, demanding kiss across her lips.

The moment he released her, Mack tugged her toward him and kissed her, too. His kiss was passionate, slow, and full of promises he didn't need to put into words.

When he finally lifted his head again, she closed her eyes and tried to detect any change within herself, but nothing seemed different. "I feel the same," she said, slightly disappointed.

"Give it a little time. It's going to take more than a minute for the nanotech to replicate and spread." Mack nipped her earlobe. "Besides, there are better things we can be doing right now than waiting for your new upgrades to kick in."

"What—" was all she managed to say before she was flat on her back looking up at her lovers' handsome faces, both of them wearing predatory smiles that made her clit throb and her breath catch in her throat.

"I want to taste you, sweetheart. It feels like forever since I've had your sweet honey on my lips," Dash said.

"Open your legs for him. Show us how ready you are for us to love you," Mack said, his tone bordering on command without going over the edge.

She parted her thighs, not even trying to hide her eagerness. It had been too long since they'd all been together like this, but that wouldn't be a problem any longer. They had an entire future stretching out before them. It was more than she had ever dared dream of, and now, it was more than a dream, it was reality.

Mack saw the dreamy smile bloom on Lieksa's lips as Dash settled into position between her legs and buried his face in her pussy and it made his cock turn to steel in a nanosecond. She was the most beautiful woman in the galaxy, and now she was theirs. It didn't matter that they hadn't had a ceremony or signed a contract yet. It wouldn't matter if they never did. They were meant to be.

He sat back to watch as Dash pleasured Lieksa with his fingers and tongue. Every soft moan and roll of her hips made him ache to be inside her, and he idly began to stroke his dick as he watched the scene playing out in front of him. This was how he wanted to spend every night from now until his dying day.

Lieksa's orgasm built to a crescendo, and she bucked and writhed on the bed. Her creamy skin was flushed, her mouth was open, her eyes glowing laser bright as she rode the crest of the wave. The scent of her arousal was all around Mack, an enticing perfume that made his mouth water. He worked his cock faster, timing his strokes to the rise of her hips.

When she finally reached release, her wild cries bounced off the walls of the cabin, nearly taking him over the edge with her. She was his every fantasy come to life, and he would never want another woman the way he wanted her.

Less than ten seconds after Dash moved back, Mack had her in his arms, rolling them both over so that she was draped over him, her legs straddling his hips and the soft mounds of her breasts pressed against his chest.

"Hi," she said as she settled herself over him, deliberately rubbing her pussy over his cock without letting him inside.

"Ready to come again?"

"Yes, please," she said before lowering her head to kiss him.

She timed the kiss so that the first swipe of her tongue across his lips happened as she reached between them to guide his cock to her entrance. Her touch made him groan, his cock throbbing in time to his heartbeat. As he slid inside her, she stared into his eyes, and he felt a sense of belonging and connection that had been missing his entire life. She was what had been missing, and making love to her was like finally coming home.

They moved together in the age-old dance that made his body hum and his blood sing in his veins. Her hands splayed over his chest, and she sat up straight, driving him deeper with every stroke. The tempo changed, growing faster and wilder. She rode him hard, and he bucked beneath her body, every give and take pushing him closer to the jagged edge of his control.

He flicked at her bouncing nipples and then let his hands move lower until his fingers were pressed against her clit and he could feel the point where their bodies joined. She started trembling, so he used his free hand to flick her sensitive nipple again. This time her body clamped around his, and she moaned, her head falling back as her control slipped another notch.

He kept pushing her toward her breaking point, and when she came it was on a shuddering cry that had him tumbling over the precipice right behind her.

She was still slumped over his chest, panting softly, when Dash chimed in.

"So, that endurance kick in yet? Or would you like a moment to recover?"

She lifted her head and gave Dash a slow, sultry smile that made Mack's cock stir despite having come only seconds before. It was the sexiest expression he'd ever seen.

"I'm ready for more."

Dash blinked. "Mack, we might be in trouble here."

"Could be. Looks like we're going to have to up our game."

She arched a brow and tossed her hair back over her shoulder in open challenge. "In that case, game on."

She gave Mack one last kiss before going into Dash's arms with an eagerness that made him laugh. She tangled her arms around his neck as he laid claim to her mouth, need driving him hard. He needed to be inside her, loving her, making her call out his name. She hung onto him as he lowered her to the mattress, kissing her until the world fell away. He covered her body with his own, and she wrapped her legs around his hips, locking them together.

Her hands stroked down his arms and back up to his shoulders before twining around his neck again. "Love me," she whispered.

"Always."

He arched his back and positioned himself, then held still as his mouth plundered hers. He wanted to stretch out this moment, to memorize every detail of her face and body. This was the beginning of their life together, and he already knew it was a memory he would always cherish. When he couldn't wait another second, he drove himself in deep, losing himself in the slick heat of her body. Need, raw and primal blended with emotions so powerful they stole his breath, and he knew part of his soul would be lost in her forever.

Her inner walls gripped his cock, milking him with every thrust and slowly shredding his control. It was a losing battle, and soon he was hammering into her, the air filled with the music of her cries and the relentless beat of their bodies coming together over and over. He wanted to hang onto these last moments, but it would have been easier to ride a comet than to stop the inevitable. Her nails raked his back, and he came harder than he'd ever done before. There were stars dancing in his vision when he finally opened his eyes again, but beyond them, he could see an even more dazzling sight; the woman he loved staring up at him with adoration glowing in her beautiful blue eyes.

"I love you so much it scared me at first," she whispered, then reached up to cup his cheek in her hand. "I'm not afraid anymore. Not of this, or of anything that might be coming our way."

"A little fear isn't a bad thing. It keeps you alive. If Dash felt a bit more of it, maybe he wouldn't get shot so often," Mack observed, placing a gentle hand on the crown of her head.

She laughed. "If Dash hadn't gotten shot, then we might never have crossed paths again. All of this was destined to happen. I know it."

"I don't care how we found each other again, I'm just glad we did." Dash couldn't imagine what their lives would be like if they'd never found their angel again, and now he would never have to. Against all the odds, she was back, and this time she was here to stay.

The End

TROUBLE DOUBLED

A short story with the characters from Double Down

Zura added a few more globs of icing to the gingerbread structure and quickly placed more of the blue and silver candies before the icing hardened. She had managed to find a decent source of gingerbread dough to load into the food dispenser, but the machine was having trouble getting the icing mixture right. There were always challenges to re-creating an old-fashioned recipe like this, but she was making it work. More or less. It had taken most of the afternoon to assemble and decorate all the pieces, and she was almost out of time. It would have gone faster if she'd asked one of her friends for help, but this was a labor of love, and she wanted to do it herself.

She worked as quickly as she could, humming an old, half-remembered holiday tune her father used to sing at this time of year, back when she was a little girl. As a child, she'd been fascinated by the lyrics and had peppered her dad with questions. What was a sleigh, and why did they make a horse pull it instead of having thrusters installed? Why did they need to put bells on the poor horse? Where were the people all dashing off to? Her dad had made up all sorts of answers to her questions, each sillier and more unlikely than the last.

As her hand rose to touch the battered family ring she wore on a chain around her neck she smiled at the memory, despite the pang of sadness that still hit every time she thought about her father. "I hope you're out there, Daddy. Watching over me like you promised. I wish you were still with us. I miss you."

She gripped the ring a little tighter. "I would give anything to have you here today, so I could see the look on your face when I share my big news."

A timer chimed, announcing the last batch of gingerbread was finished being processed by the food dispenser. She had intentionally made more than she needed because she knew if she didn't have extras to feed to Kit and Luke, they would likely devour her creation before it was finished. After all her hard work, she wasn't going to let that happen.

It had taken a few days to get everything organized, and hours of planning to work out how to create a gingerbread version of Nova Club where they all worked and lived. Back when she'd done this with her dad, every year they would make a replica of their ship, the Sun Sprite. It was the only home she had ever known—until now.

These days, her home was Nova on Astek Station, and her heart belonged to her husbands, Kit and Luke. In the months since their wedding, everything had fallen into place. Business at the club continued to thrive, and her new business running luxury goods and precious cargo out to the Drift was off to a strong start. She had four pilots signed on, including her brother, Royan, and her friend, Phyl Harrington, each of them with their own ship. She was building more than a business out here in the dark reaches of the galaxy. She was building a future for herself, and her family.

Zura set the gingerbread out to cool, picked up the icing, and returned to the task of decorating the group of gingerbread figures laid out in front of her.

She was still working on them when the door opened.

"Holy *fraxx*, what smells so good?" Luke called out.

"Haven't you ever had gingerbread before?" she asked in response.

"I have, and I know it didn't taste half as good as that smells. Hey, gorgeous, you look sexy, and very sticky." Luke appeared in the kitchen, scooping her into his arms for a kiss that made her toes curl. "Yep. Sticky, sweet, and very tasty."

"What's all this? Did you decide to open a bakery while we were at work?" Kit asked, gesturing around the small area that functioned as their kitchen. Every inch of counter space was taken up with candies, bowls of tinted icing, and racks of gingerbread, while the table was taken over by the gingerbread and confection creation she'd spent the day working on.

"Nope. Not a bakery. Just a little something my dad and I used to do to celebrate the Festival of Light."

"I thought you two weren't much for traditional holidays?" Luke said as he released her.

She went from Luke's arms to Kit's as her other husband moved in for a kiss of his own. "You taste amazing. If this is the holiday tradition, I'm all for it."

"No, I'm not the tradition, that is." She laughed and pointed her icing covered spatula in the direction of her gingerbread version of the Nova. "Tada!"

"Is that—"

"It's Nova! Check it out, Kit. She's even got the fight cage in here," Luke was leaning over the table, eyeing everything with interest.

"Dad and I used to build a gingerbread house every year. It was something he'd done with his mother, all the way back through the generations. We'd bake, and eat icing and candy, and sing old holiday songs. He said it was important to celebrate family, and remember that no matter how dark the night got, the light would always come back into the world eventually."

"That's a lovely sentiment, little one. But uh, I'm quite certain what you've made there is not a house," Kit pointed out. He kept an arm draped around her waist as he admired her handiwork.

"No, it's not. But the Nova is my home, just like the Sun Sprite used to be."

"I like this tradition." Kit pulled her in close and kissed her again. "Next year, maybe we can do it together? Like a family."

"I'd like that."

"Hey, I found people. Are these supposed to be us?" Luke asked, holding up the figures decorated to look a little like himself and his twin brother.

"I wasn't finished setting everything up. The three of us go inside the club." She pointed to a spot near the bar.
"This must be you," Kit said, picking up another figure, this one covered in blue icing.

"And these must be extras." Luke picked up the last two decorated gingerbread figures, both of them barely a quarter of the size of the others. "Snack sized!"

"Don't you dare eat those!" She smacked Luke's wrist with her spatula, sending frosting in all directions.
"Okay, okay, not eating the delicious little people-shaped cookies. Can I ask why not?"

Zura's pulse raced and her stomach filled with butterflies the size of small asteroids. It was time to tell them. "Because they belong in the club next to the figures of the three of us."

Both men looked at her with quizzical expressions. "Who are they supposed to be?"

She moved in, taking the pieces from Luke and arranging them inside the club, the three adults leaning up against the bar, with the smaller figures nestled at their feet.

"They don't have names yet. We've got about seven months to rectify that." She smiled up at them and placed a hand on her stomach. "Those are your children. I got confirmation from Alyson a couple of days ago. I'm pregnant."

"Holy *fraxx*, babies!" Luke exclaimed, grinning from ear to ear.

"Two?" Kit asked, his voice barely above a whisper.

"Twins, just like their fathers," she confirmed.

"I'm going to be a father," Kit said, every word uttered slowly, as if he didn't quite believe the words coming out of his mouth.

"We're going to be fathers. *Re'veth*. We're going to be in charge of raising tiny, helpless humans." Luke shook his head, then walked over to her, sank to his knees, and leaned in to press his head to her stomach. "I've never been so excited and terrified in my entire life."

"Me either," Kit said.

"None of us had normal upbringings, but we'll figure this out, together. That's what we talked about when we decided to try for a family, right?"

she reminded them, her fingers stroking Luke's brow.

"Nothing about our lives has ever been normal. I don't think it matters. We're going to love our kids and do our best to protect them. That's all any parent can do." Kit hugged her and nuzzled his face into her hair. "You are going to be the sexiest mom the galaxy has ever seen."

"Hell yeah," Luke agreed, pressing a kiss to her tummy. "You hear that, little guys? You've got the prettiest, most amazing mom any kid could hope for."

She patted Luke's head. "You know, they might not be little guys at all. They could be little girls."

Both men groaned at the thought.

"If you're carrying our daughters, we're doomed. They'll have your silver eyes and gorgeous blue hair and we'll be wrapped around their tiny fingers before they've spoken their first words," Kit murmured.

"Yep. You don't know yet, do you, gorgeous? I mean, if they're girls or boys?"

She shook her head. "I thought we'd want to find out together. I have another appointment at the medical center in a few days."

"Nothing's wrong, though? You're okay? *Veth*, should you have spent all this time on your feet? Shouldn't you be resting or something? Pregnant women need a lot of rest, right? And food. You're eating for three now!" Kit grabbed a piece of gingerbread and handed it to her. "Eat this. You have to keep your strength up."

She was laughing as she took a bite, then another. When it was gone, she said, "I'm fine. The babies are fine. I'm going to need more rest, yes. But I have your medi-bots keeping me healthy, remember?"

Both men stilled. "That's going to be a problem, isn't it?" Luke asked, but it wasn't really a question. They knew the answer already. The corporations that had created the cyborgs never intended for them to be freed from service. They were made to fight and die in the Resource Wars. They were the perfect soldiers, designed to fight better and longer than any human, without ever questioning an order or expecting payment. After the war ended and the cyborgs revealed that they were self-aware, the corporations were forced to free them.

What the corporations hadn't told anyone was that they secretly administered something to every surviving female cyborg to ensure they couldn't conceive. They had to. It was the only way to stop the nanobots every cyborg carried from being introduced into the civilian population. If the cyborg females ever conceived, their offspring would be born with their mother's medi-bots in their bloodstream. The corporations were determined to stop that from happening, but Zura was a complication they hadn't foreseen. When Kit and Luke had saved her life by introducing their own medi-bots into her system, they had inadvertently created a problem for the corporations. Any child of Zura's would carry their mother's nanotech, and there was nothing the corporations could do about it. At least, not legally.

Legalities wouldn't stop the corporations from trying to interfere.

"Whatever they try, we'll be ready for them. Dr. Jefferies sent copies of all my medical files off-station. If something happens, they'll be released to the intergalactic newsgroups, along with her reports."

Kit growled. "Nothing is going to happen to you or our children, little one. We won't let them near you."

"I know," she said. She meant it, too. Luke and Kit were her life, and she was theirs. There was nothing they wouldn't do for each other, or for their growing family.

"I love you, little one."

Kit's words made her smile, and she looked up to find him staring at her in utter adoration. He stroked her cheek and then pulled her in for a slow, lingering kiss. Luke caught her hand and drew it down to his lips, nibbling and licking at her icing-coated fingertips.

"Love you, too. My tasty little wife," Luke said before sucking her finger into his mouth.

Before she knew it, both men were working together to strip her out of her clothes. "You know I still consider it cheating when you two talk between yourselves via that internal channel thing you have."

"We know, but it makes coordinating seductions so much easier," Kit replied.

She felt something cool touch her hip and looked down in time to see Luke slicing off her panties with the knife she'd been using to cut the gingerbread. "That's not even a little bit sanitary," she pointed out with a laugh.

"I promise to do the dishes and sanitize everything later."

"So, I get orgasms, and you do the dishes? I like this arrangement," she stuck her hip out to give him easier access.

"Whatever you want, gorgeous."

He finished removing her underwear and then tossed the knife so it landed point first into the nearest wall. Before she could comment on the damage, he stroked his hands up her thighs, successfully distracting her. Her pussy flooded with arousal as he stared at her with a look of brazen hunger she would never grow tired of seeing. He buried his face between her thighs and she reached back to hang onto Kit as a wave of pleasure washed over her, leaving her weak-kneed and unsteady.

"I've got you," Kit said.

"And you always will," she answered.

Kit held her as Luke lifted her legs over his shoulders and started eating her pussy with eager strokes and soft groans. She was suspended between them, unable to do anything except enjoy the erotic sensation of being devoured. It didn't take long for her to reach the jagged edge of her control, and when he slid a finger into her channel she exploded like a meteor on re-entry.

"You are breathtaking, little one. No matter how long we're together, I will always love seeing you like this," Kit said as the two of them eased her still trembling body to the floor.

She stretched out and got comfortable as the two of them stripped quickly. She loved seeing their hard, muscled bodies naked. Her two gorgeous cyborgs, the men she had once only dreamed of having in her bed. Now, they were her *vardo*, her lifemates and the fathers of her children.

"You stay right there," Luke told her as he reached for a half-full bowl of frosting. It was the blue tinted one she had used to create her own figure, as well as decorate the walls of the gingerbread version of the bar.

"What are you going to do?" she asked, more focused on watching the flex and play of muscles across Luke's chest than what he was doing.

"Finger-painting. Kids like this kind of thing, right? We should get some practice in before they're born," Kit said with a chuckle, reaching for another bowl.

"Yep. We're going to paint your beautiful body with this, then lick it all over. Sound like a plan, gorgeous?"

"It sounds like a mess. But since I'm pregnant, you two wouldn't expect me to scrub the floors, so I'm game."

They were true to their word. As she lay on the warm floor, the two of them took turns painting her breasts, stomach, and thighs with different colors of frosting; licking it off as it started to harden. Soon she was on fire from head to toe, craving more than the light touches and nibbles they grazed along her skin. She needed them inside her, the three of them bound together, body and soul.

"I want you," she whispered, and they responded so quickly she knew they were feeling the same way.

They guided her to her hands and knees, Luke kneeling in front of her as Kit moved in behind, nudging her legs apart to make room for himself. Luke kissed her as Kit positioned his thick cock at her entrance, sliding inside with a low, guttural groan of raw need.

Hands gripped her hips, holding her steady against the pounding rhythm of Kit's thrusts. Luke ended their kiss with a light nip to her lower lip, rising on his knees so that his cock was jutting up a few inches from her mouth. She bent her head and opened wide, taking him deep inside. Luke's fingers tangled in her hair, and she let Kit's movement push her forward with each thrust of his hips.

She was linked to both of them, every move they made relayed through her to the other brother. Time slowed, and the world fell away until it was only the three of them, locked together in an intricate dance of give and take.

It wasn't long until the pleasure began to build to an exquisite breaking point, and when she came this time, she gripped her inner walls around Kit's cock, making sure she took him with her over the edge. He groaned her name as he came, burying himself to the hilt inside her body. She reached up to cup Luke's balls in her hand, toying with them gently in the way she knew he liked. His fingers tightened in her hair, and he whispered her name as his cock jerked in her mouth and he came, too.

She couldn't think of a better way to celebrate her news. The three of them tangled up together, breathless and happy.

Later, after they'd showered away the sweet, sticky mess they'd made of each other, she found herself back in the kitchen. She was wrapped in their arms again as the three of them looked at her gingerbread creation, complete with the tiny family nestled in the middle.

"You've given us everything we've ever dreamed of, little one. A home, love, a future, and now, a family," Kit said.

Luke nodded. "We're going to need to reconfigure this place again to add a room for our kids. It's a good thing Royan isn't here too much—

we'll take over his quarters and give him space in the employee section."

"Uncle Royan will probably decide to stay on the Sun Sprite when we tell him. He's already convinced love is some kind of contagious condition that dooms everyone who catches it. Once he finds out about the babies, he'll likely volunteer for every long-haul trip to the far side of the galaxy."

"He's wrong, you know, sweetheart. Falling in love doesn't mean you're doomed. It's the start of something incredible." Luke pressed a kiss to the top of her head.

"I think so, too." Zura melted into their embrace, letting the warmth of their love wrap around her like a cocoon. She was the luckiest woman in all the worlds. No matter what the future brought, she knew they would face it together, as a family.

THE END

ABOUT THE AUTHOR

Susan lives out on the Canadian west coast surrounded by open water, dear family, and good friends. She's jumped out of perfectly good airplanes on purpose and accidently swum with sharks on the Great Barrier Reef.

If the world ends, she plans to survive as the spunky, comedic sidekick to the heroes of the new world, because she's too damned short and out of shape to make it on her own for long.

To contact her about her books or to arrange end of the world team-ups, you can email her at *susan@susanhayes.ca.*

For all titles by Susan Hayes, please visit her website: **susanhayes.ca**

To keep up with her latest news, releases, and appearances you can join her Newsletter: http://eepurl.com/bd_GoH

THE DRIFT SERIES

Double Down

All in

Wild Card

Three of a Kind

www.ingramcontent.com/pod-product-compliance
Lightning Source LLC
Chambersburg PA
CBHW061610190726
48288CB00007B/2263